Big Apple

Street Smarts

Big Apple

Street Smarts

Names, Addresses, Phone Numbers & Information

Enabling You To Survive Smart In Manhattan

THE CONSULTANT PRESS,LTD.
NEW YORK, NEW YORK

PUBLISHED BY:
THE CONSULTANT PRESS, LTD.
163 AMSTERDAM AVENUE
NEW YORK, NEW YORK 10023
(212) 838-8640

Robert S. Persky, Editor

Ewan K. Campbell, Associate Research Editor

ISBN: 0-913069-33-7

LIBRARY OF CONGRESS CATALOG CARD NUMBER: 91-92503

Distributed by: Career Press
180 Fifth Ave.
Hawthorne, NJ 07507
1-800-CAREER-1
FAX 201-427-2037

TABLE OF CONTENTS

PREFACE

*The buildings were constant flames, bright
and shining . . . and the people on the street
below were the people that built that fire
and kept it alive . . . seven million Keepers
of the Flame. The sound of traffic on a New
York street creates a strange music. It is an
orchestra conducted by the Statue of Liberty,
with the words engraved forever on her side
. . . I opened my tower windows wide to let
the music in.*

More than forty years have elapsed since Gordon
Jenkins penned the words and music of his ode to
Manhattan. There are those who, with some justification,
claim that The Big Apple is no longer a city of light and
wonder.

There are others, the editor of this volume included,
who remain "Keepers of the Flame." Manhattan continues
to offer the largest variety in theater, movies, music,
museums, restaurants, business, conventions, and street
life. Towers continue to rise and illuminate the night.

Part of the wonder of Manhattan is based on the fact
that the City never sleeps. In no other city can one find as
many resources which are open 7 days a week, and, in
some instances, 24 hours a day. Taxis and subways carry
their passengers throughout the night.

Manhattan, like the Statute of Liberty, continues to
nurture its residents and beckon business visitors and
tourists. *Big Apple Street Smarts* was created to assist
residents, business visitors, and tourists in finding and
using the resources of Manhattan. It is not a travel guide.
It is a resource book designed for living smart!

New York, New York

Robert S. Persky
Editor

HOW TO USE BIG APPLE STREET SMARTS

The arrangement of the information contained in *Big Apple Street Smarts* is at the whim of the editor.

Since I can't commence any activity without music, the first topic is *The City Listens*, a guide to the radio stations heard in the Big Apple. I think Gordon Jenkins would approve.

After using this guide for a few minutes you will become familiar with the topics and their sequence. Until then, commence your search for the information you desire by referring to the Table Of Contents or the extensive Index.

When it is important to know an address, the address is included. If the key to obtaining the service, information, or reaching someone is a phone number, only the phone number is listed. For example, if you need an all night copy shop you will require an address. On the other hand, to summon a locksmith at 3am to open your front door, you need only a phone number.

One of the wonders of Manhattan is that it is not static. Businesses and institutions established during the Civil War have foundered and disappeared in the '80s. As the demand for telephone service increases, new exchanges are added and often a government agency or business firm changes its telephone number without changing its address. Always call to verify that the place you desire to visit is still in business and at the same address.

THE CITY LISTENS

♪ Finding Your Spot On The Dial

Big Apple Street Smarts: Manhattan generates its own music. From street musician to subway concert, you are rarely distant from music chosen by someone else. Your work and play will be enhanced by your favorite sound. Find a spot on the dial that belongs to you. If you are a consumer of news you can choose an all news station!

The Editor's Picks:

ALL NEWS ● WINS   BIG BAND ● WNEW
CLASSICAL ● WQXR   CONTEMPORARY HITS ● WPLJ
COUNTRY ● WYNY   EASY LISTENING ● WPAT
JAZZ ● WBGO   ROCK ● WBAB
SOFT ROCK ● WNSR

Where to find your spot.

WABC
Frequency: 770 AM
Format: Talk/News

WADO
Frequency: 1280 AM
Format: Spanish Language

WALK-AM
Frequency: 1370 AM
Format: Adult Contemporary

WALK-FM
Frequency: 97.5 FM
Format: Adult Contemporary

WBAB-AM
Frequency: 1240 AM
Format: New/Rock

WBAB-FM
Frequency: 102.3
Format: Rock

WBAI
Frequency: 99.5 FM
Format: Varied

WBAZ
Frequency: 101.7 FM
Format: Light Contemporary

WBGO
Frequency: 88.3 FM
Format: Jazz

WBLI
Frequency: 106.1 FM
Format: Adult Contemporary

WBLS
Frequency: 107.5 FM
Format: Urban Contemp.

WCBS - AM
Frequency: 880 AM
Format: All news

WCBS - FM
Frequency: 101.1 FM
Format: Oldies

WCTO
Frequency: 94.3 FM
Format: Easy Listening

WCWP
Frequency: 88.1 FM
Format: Classical/Jazz

WDHA
Frequency: 105.5 FM
Format: Rock

WDRE
Frequency: 92.7 FM
Format: Progressive Rock

WEBE
Frequency 107.9 FM
Format: Adult Contemporary

WEVD
Frequency: 1050 AM
Format: Big Band/Nostalgia

WEZN
Frequency: 99.9 FM
Format: Easy Listening

WFAN
Frequency: 660 AM
Format: Sports

WFDU
Frequency: 89.1 FM
Format: Music/Public Radio

WFMU
Frequency: 91.1 FM
Format: Varied

WFUV
Frequency: 90.7 FM
Format: Fordham University

WGSM
Frequency: 740 AM
Format: Big Band/Nostalgia

WHFM
Frequency: 95.3 FM
Format: Adult Contemporary

WHLI
Frequency: 1100 AM
Format: Oldies

WHTZ
Frequency: 100.3 FM
Format: Top 40

WHUD
Frequency 100.7 FM
Format: Easy Listening

WICC
Frequency: 600 AM
Format: Adult Contemporary

WINS
Frequency: 1010 AM
Format: All news

WKCR
Frequency: 89.8 FM
Format: Columbia University

WKJY
Frequency: 98.3 FM
Format: Adult Contemporary

WLIB
Frequency: 1190 AM
Format: Talk/Caribbean

WLIM
Frequency: 1580 AM
Format: Big Bands/Talk

WLNG
Frequency: 92.1 FM
Format: Oldies/Contemp.

WLTW
Frequency: 106.7 FM
Format: Light Contemporary

WMCA
Frequency: 570 AM
Format: Talk/News

WMTR
Frequency: 1250 AM
Format: Talk/News

WNCN
Frequency: 104.3 FM
Format: Classical

WNEW-AM
Frequency: 1130 AM
Format: Adult Stnds./Sports

WNEW-FM
Frequency: 102.7 FM
Format: Rock

WNSR
Frequency: 105.1 FM
Format: Soft rock

WNYC-AM
Frequency: 820 AM
Format: NYC News/Talk

WNYC-FM
Frequency: 93.9 FM
Format: Classical

WNYE
Frequency: 91.5 FM
Format: Community Svcs.

WNYG
Frequency: 1440 AM
Format: Music

WOR
Frequency: 710 AM
Format: Talk/News

WPAT-AM
Frequency: 930 AM
Format: Easy Listening

WPAT-FM
Frequency: 93.1 FM
Format: Easy Listening

WPLJ
Frequency: 95.5 FM
Format: Top 40

WPLR
Frequency: 99.1 FM
Format: Comedy/Rock

WPSC
Frequency: 88.7 FM
Format: Top 40

WQCD
Frequency: 101.9 FM
Format: Contemporary Jazz

WQHT
Frequency: 97.1 FM
Format: Top 40/Urban

WQQQ
Frequency 96.7 FM
Format: Oldies

WQXR-AM
Frequency: 1560 AM
Format: Classical

WQXR-FM
Frequency: 96.3 FM
Format: Classical

WRCN
Frequency: 103.9 FM
Format: Rock

WRHD
Frequency: 1570 AM
Format: Nostalgia

WRKS
Frequency: 98.7 FM
Format: Urban Contemp.

WRTN
Frequency: 93.5 FM
Format: Big Band/Nostalgia

WVOX
Frequency: 1460 AM
Format: Talk/Nostalgia

WWDJ
Frequency: 970 AM
Format: Christian Music

WWHB
Frequency: 107.1 FM
Format: Top 40

WWRL
Frequency: 1600 AM
Format: Gospel Music

WWRV
Frequency: 1330 AM
Format: Ethnic

WXRK
Frequency: 92.3 FM
Format: Classical Rock

WYNY
Frequency: 103.5 FM
Format: Country

WZRC
Frequency: 1480 AM
Format: Hard Rock

PHONE SMARTS

☎ Information

Big Apple Street Smarts: It will costs you 45¢ in the Big Apple for each inquiry relating to a local number dialed from your home, office, or hotel room. It's free from the public phone in the lobby or on the street. Information relating to toll free lines is free regardless of which phone you use.

Nationwide Toll Free Numbers ☎ 800-555-1212
Manhattan & Bronx Numbers ☎ 411
Brooklyn-Queens-Staten Island ☎ 555-1212
Outside NYC ☎ 1 + Area Code + 555-1212

13

Beware of hotel room phone charges!

Even though you intend to use your own long distance calling card to call from your hotel, a charge may be imposed by the hotel for the local call to the connecting exchange. The charge may be imposed even if the call itself is toll free from a public phone or your office or home. The charge may be as high as $1.00 and at luxury hotels may even exceed that amount.

Big Apple Street Smarts: If the hotel charges for "toll free" calls, make your calls from the public phones in the lobby.

What's the phone number I'm at?

Big Apple Street Smarts: If you're at a phone where the number is missing or defaced, dial 958. You will be told the phone number of the phone you are using. You get your coin back if it is a pay phone. If you are short of change, and the number is missing, obtain the number before you make your call. Then you can give your party the number so they may call you back.

Which Long Distance Carrier?

Dial 1-700-555-4141 and a recording will tell you which long distance carrier your phone is connected to.

Big Apple Street Smarts: Beware of the charges if it is not AT&T, MCI, Sprint, or your own special carrier.

Numbers That Alert You To Calls That Cost Extra.

Big Apple Street Smarts: Exchanges that begin with any of the following three numbers belong to information providers that charge you for each call. The New York Telephone company is not affiliated with the providers and does not provide the messages. It does not regulate the cost of the calls.

☎ 394   ☎ 900
☎ 540   ☎ 970
☎ 550   ☎ 976
☎ 700

Big Apple Street Smarts: If you desire to stop persons in your home making calls to any of these services, you should request blocking service. Blocking restricts outgoing calls from your telephone to some or all of these information service numbers. Blocking service is provided at no charge to residence customers but you must request it!

Your Motor Vehicle May Be Unsafe!

A complete list of recall notices for cars, trucks and vans, is obtainable by using your touch-tone phone. Information will be mailed to you within a week. Know your make, model and year when you call. The information is free. ☎ 202-366-0123

If Your Credit Card Is Lost Or Stolen

American Express	☎ 800-528-4800
AT&T	☎ 800-222-0300
Diners Club	☎ 800-525-9135
Discover	☎ 800-347-2683
enRoute	☎ 800-367-6883
MasterCard	☎ 800-826-2181
Visa	☎ 800-336-8472

If Your Travelers Checks Are Lost Or Stolen

American Express	☎ 800-528-4800
MasterCard	☎ 800-223-9920
Visa	☎ 800-227-6811

Travel & Transportation Information

Big Apple Street Smarts: The names given below are those used by Manhattanites. We never heard anyone refer to La Guardia Airport as La Guardia International Airport!

Amtrak	☎ 800-872-7245
Bus Terminal - Port Authority	☎ 564-8484
Kennedy Airport	☎ 718-656-4520
La Guardia Airport	☎ 718-476-5000
Long Island Railroad	☎ 718-217-5477
Metro North Railroad	☎ 532-4900
Metro Transportation Authority	☎ 878-7000
Metroliner	☎ 800-523-8720
New Jersey Transit	☎ 201-935-2500
Newark Airport	☎ 201-961-2000
PATH (The Tubes)	☎ 201-460-8444
Transit Authority - Bus/Subway Info.	☎ 718-330-1234

Toll-Free Numbers For Airlines, Hotel & Motel Chains, And Discount Travel

Big Apple Street Smarts: When calling from a public phone or even your home phone, local calls add up. Use toll free numbers. You may even find better service since sophisticated systems are used to keep the toll free lines from being clogged with busy signals.

Airlines

Some airlines do not offer toll free numbers to call their local office. If there is no toll-free number listed for the airline you want to reach, refer to the Manhattan phone book.

Big Apple Street Smarts: If you have the time, making your reservation directly may result in the best fare. Travel agents vary from super to incompetent. Generally the earlier you reserve the better. Discounts tend to be granted when making reservations 30 days or 21 days in advance. Senior citizen discounts commence at 62 and may apply to your traveling companion regardless of age. If you don't ask, you won't get the discount.

AEROLINEAS ARGENTINAS	☎ 800-225-9920
AEROMEXICO	☎ 800-237-6639
AEROPERU AIRLINES	☎ 800-255-7378
AERO CALIFORNIA	☎ 800-258-3311
AIR CANADA AIRLINES	☎ 800-776-3000
AIR FRANCE	☎ 800-237-2747
AIR INDIA	☎ 800-223-2250
AIR JAMAICA	☎ 800-523-5585
AIR NEVADA	☎ 800-634-6377
AIR NEW ZEALAND	☎ 800-421-5913
AIR PACIFIC	☎ 800-354-7471
AIR PANAMA INTERNATIONAL	☎ 800-272-6262
ALASKA AIRLINES	☎ 800-426-0333
ALIA ROYAL JORDANIAN AIR.	☎ 800-442-8485
ALITALIA AIRLINES, New York	☎ 800-223-5730
ALM ANTILLEAN AIRLINES	☎ 800-327-7230
ALOHA AIRLINES	☎ 800-367-5250
AMERICAN AIRLINES	☎ 800-433-7300
AMERICAN TRANS AIR	☎ 800-225-2995
AMERICA WEST AIRLINES	☎ 800-247-5692
AUSTRIAN AIRLINES	☎ 800-843-0002
AVIANCA AIRLINES	☎ 800-284-2622
AVIATECA GUATEMALA AIR.	☎ 800-327-9832
BRITISH AIRWAYS	☎ 800-247-9297
BWIA INTERNATIONAL AIR.	☎ 800-327-7401
CANADIAN AIRLINES	☎ 800-426-7000
CANADIAN HOLIDAYS	☎ 800-282-4751
CAYMAN AIRWAYS	☎ 800-441-3003
CHINA AIRLINES	☎ 800-227-5118
CONTINENTAL AIRLINES	☎ 800-525-0280

DELTA AIRLINES	☎ 800-221-1212
DIRECT AIR	☎ 800-428-0706
DOMINICANA AIRLINES	☎ 800-327-7240
ECUATORIANA AIRLINE	☎ 800-328-2367
EGYPT AIR	☎ 800-334-6787
ETHIOPIAN AIRLINES	☎ 800-443-9677
FAUCETT PERUVIAN AIR.	☎ 800-334-3356
FINNAIR	☎ 800-950-5000
HAWAIIAN AIRLINES	☎ 800-367-5320
HORIZON AIR	☎ 800-547-9308
HUNGARIAN AIRLINES	☎ 800-877-5429
IBERIA AIR LINES OF SPAIN	☎ 800-772-4642
ICELANDAIR	☎ 800-223-5500
JAPAN AIR LINES	☎ 800-525-3663
KLM ROYAL DUTCH AIRLINES	☎ 800-777-5553
KOREAN AIR LINES	☎ 800-421-8200
KUWAIT AIRWAYS	☎ 800-458-9248
LAN CHILE AIRLINES	☎ 800-735-5526
LAS VEGAS AIRLINES	☎ 800-634-6851
LACSA AIRLINES	☎ 800-225-2272
LINEAS AEREAS PARAGUAYAS	☎ 800-327-5577
LLOYD AEREO BOLIVIANO AIR.	☎ 800-327-7407
LUFTHANSA	☎ 800-645-3880
MALAYSIAN AIRLINES	☎ 800-421-8641
MEXICANA AIRLINES	☎ 800-531-7921
MGM GRAND AIR	☎ 800-933-2646
NEW YORK HELICOPTER	☎ 800-645-3494
NORTHWEST AIRLINES	☎ 800-225-2525
PARADISE ISLAND AIR	☎ 800-432-8807
PHILIPPINE AIRLINES	☎ 800-435-9725
QANTAS AIRWAYS	☎ 800-227-4500
SABENA BELGIAN WORLD AIR.	☎ 800-955-2000
SAS SCANDINAVIAN AIRLINES	☎ 800-221-2350
SCENIC AIRLINES	☎ 800-634-6801
SINGAPORE AIRLINES	☎ 800-742-3333
SOUTH AFRICAN AIRWAYS	☎ 800-722-9675
SOUTHWEST AIRLINES	☎ 800-531-5601
SURINAM AIRWAYS	☎ 800-327-6864
SWISSAIR	☎ 800-221-4750
TACA INTERNATIONAL AIR.	☎ 800-535-8780
TAN-SAHSA AIRLINES	☎ 800-327-1225
TAP-AIR PORTUGAL	☎ 800-221-7370
THAI AIRWAYS	☎ 800-426-5204
TRANS BRAZIL AIRLINES	☎ 800-872-3153
TRANS WORLD AIR. (TWA)	☎ 800-221-2000
UNITED AIRLINES,	☎ 800-241-6522
USAIR	☎ 800-428-4322
VARIG BRAZILIAN AIRLINES	☎ 800-468-2744
VIASA VENEZUELA AIRLINES	☎ 800-327-5454
VIRGIN AIR	☎ 800-522-3084
YEMEN AIRWAYS	☎ 800-257-1133
YUGOSLAV AIRLINES	☎ 800-752-6528
ZAMBIA AIRWAYS	☎ 800-223-1136

Automobile Rentals & Leasing

Big Apple Street Smarts: Almost all rental companies require that you have a major credit card. Cash is out except for payment when you return the car. Several credit cards cover, without extra charge, collision insurance. That benefit is particularly valuable if you don't own a car and therefore have your own insurance. You save big bucks by declining the rental company's insurance and relying on the plan offered by your credit card company.

There are many good local companies with competitive rates. Listed below are a few of the major national and regional rental companies.

AJAX RENT-A-CAR	☎ 800-562-5277
ALAMO RENT-A-CAR	☎ 800-327-9633
AMERICAN INT. RENT-A-CAR	☎ 800-527-0202
AUTO HOST CAR RENTALS	☎ 800-448-4678
AVIS RENT-A-CAR	☎ 800-331-1212
BUDGET RENT-A-CAR	☎ 800-527-0700
DOLLAR RENT-A-CAR	☎ 800-421-6868
EURORENT USA	☎ 800-521-2235
GENERAL RENT-A-CAR	☎ 800-327-7607
NATIONAL CAR RENTAL SYS.	☎ 800-227-7368
PAYLESS CAR RENTAL SYS.	☎ 800-237-2804
RENT-A-WRECK	☎ 800-535-1391
THRIFTY RENT-A-CAR	☎ 800-367-2277

Discount Travel Services

Big Apple Street Smarts: If you are able to pickup and leave on short notice, the discount plans offer major savings on cruises, tours, and foreign air travel. Some discounters require "membership", while others will deal with you on a trip by trip basis. Try to pay by credit card. It protects you in the event the travel agent or tour operator doesn't survive.

AMBASSADOR SATELLITE	☎ 800-235-5800
AMBASSADOR TOURS	☎ 800-346-3592
BREAKAWAY CLUB	☎ 800-872-8364
CONCIERGE, Denver	☎ 800-346-1022
CRUISE ADVISORS	☎ 800-544-9361
CRUISE AND LEISURE TRAVEL	☎ 800-423-8271
CRUISE PRO	☎ 800-222-7447
CRUISE STARS	☎ 800-732-7287
DISCOUNT TRAVEL INT.	☎ 800-334-9294
ENCORE TRAVEL CLUB	☎ 800-638-0930
ENTERTAINMENT PUBL.	☎ 800-521-9640
GOLDEN AGE TRAVELLERS	☎ 800-258-8880
GRAND CIRCLE TRAVEL	☎ 800-221-2610
HIDEAWAYS INTERNATIONAL	☎ 800-843-4433
LAST MINUTE TRAVEL	☎ 800-527-8646

RESERVATIONS PLUS	☎ 800-422-7580
SAGA INTERNATIONAL	☎ 800-343-0273
SOUTH FLORIDA CRUISES	☎ 800-327-7447
SPUR OF THE MOMENT CR.	☎ 800-343-1991
STAND BUYS LIMITED	☎ 800-255-0200
THE CRUISE LINE	☎ 800-327-3021
TRANS NAT.-LAST MINUTE TR.	☎ 800-262-0123
TRAVEL AVENUE	☎ 800-333-3335
TRAVEL BOUND	☎ 800-456-2005
TRAVEL CHANNEL CLUB	☎ 800-872-8355
TRAVELER'S ADVANTAGE	☎ 800-548-1116
UNITRAVEL	☎ 800-325-2222
UP 'N GO TRAVEL	☎ 800-888-8190
VACATIONS TO GO	☎ 800-338-4962
WHITE TRAVEL SERVICE	☎ 800-547-4790
WORLD WIDE CRUISES	☎ 800-882-9000

Hotels & Motels

AMBASSADOR INNS	☎ 800-538-1600
AMERICANA HOTELS CORP.	☎ 800-433-5677
AMFAC RESORTS, INC.	☎ 800-227-1117
ARISTOCRAT INNS	☎ 800-621-6909
BEST INNS OF AMERICA	☎ 800-237-8466
BEST WESTERN INT.	☎ 800-528-1234
BRECKENRIDGE HOTEL CORP.	☎ 800-451-5464
BUDGETEL INNS	☎ 800-428-3438
BUDGET HOST INNS	☎ 800-283-4678
CANADIAN PACIFIC HOTELS	☎ 800-828-7447
CARIBBEAN HOTEL MGT.	☎ 800-327-8165
CHOICE HOTELS	☎ 800-252-7466
COMFORT INNS INT.	☎ 800-228-5150
COURTYARD BY MARRIOTT	☎ 800-321-2211
CUNARD HOTELS & RESORTS	☎ 800-222-0939
DAYS INNS OF AMERICA	☎ 800-325-2525
DOUBLETREE HOTELS, INC.	☎ 800-528-0444
DOWNTOWNER, ROWNTOWNER AND	
PASSPORT MOTOR INNS	☎ 800-238-6161
DRURY INNS	☎ 800-325-8300
ECONOMY INNS OF AMERICA	☎ 800-826-0778
ECONO LODGES OF AMERICA	☎ 800-446-6900
EMBASSY SUITES	☎ 800-362-2779
EXEL INNS OF AMERICA	☎ 800-356-8013
FAIRFIELD INN BY MARRIOTT	☎ 800-228-2800
FAIRMONT HOTELS	☎ 800-527-4727
FAMILY INNS OF AMERICA	☎ 800-251-9752
FOUR SEASONS HOTELS	☎ 800-332-3442
FRIENDSHIP INNS INT.	☎ 800-453-4511
GUEST QUARTERS HOTELS	☎ 800-424-2900
HARLEY HOTELS	☎ 800-321-2323
HELMSLEY HOTELS	☎ 800-221-4982
HERSHEY HOTELS & RESORTS	☎ 800-437-7439
HILTON INTERNATIONAL	☎ 800-445-8667
HOLIDAY INNS	☎ 800-465-4329
HYATT CORPORATION	☎ 800-233-1234

INTER-CONTINENTAL-FORUM	☎ 800-327-0200
KOALA INNS OF AMERICA	☎ 800-325-2525
LA QUINTA MOTOR INNS	☎ 800-531-5900
LOEWS HOTELS	☎ 800-223-0888
MARRIOTT HOTELS & RESORTS	☎ 800-228-9290
MASTER ECONOMY INNS	☎ 800-633-3434
MASTER HOSTS INNS	☎ 800-251-1962
MERIDIEN HOTELS	☎ 800-543-4300
NIKKO HOTELS	☎ 800-645-5687
NOVOTEL	☎ 800-221-4542
OMNI INTERNATIONAL	☎ 800-843-6664
OUTRIGGER HOTELS	☎ 800-733-7777
PARK SUITES HOTELS	☎ 800-432-7272
PASSPORT INNS	☎ 800-238-6161
QUALITY INTERNATIONAL	☎ 800-228-5151
RADISSON HOTEL CORP.	☎ 800-333-3333
RAINTREE INNS OF AMERICA	☎ 800-843-8240
RAMADA INNS	☎ 800-228-2828
RED CARPET INNS	☎ 800-251-1962
RED LION INNS	☎ 800-547-8010
RESORTS INTERNAT. HOTELS	☎ 800-321-3000
RITZ CARLTON HOTELS	☎ 800-241-3333
ROCKRESORTS, INC.	☎ 800-223-7637
RODEWAY INNS	☎ 800-228-2000
SELECT INNS OF AMERICA	☎ 800-641-1000
SHERATON HOTELS AND INNS	☎ 800-325-3535
SOFITEL HOTELS	☎ 800-221-4542
SONESTA HOTELS	☎ 800-766-3782
TRAVELODGE INTERNATIONAL	☎ 800-255-3050
TREADWAY HOTELS	☎ 800-873-2392
TRUSTHOUSE FORTE HOTELS	☎ 800-255-3050
VAGABOND INNS	☎ 800-522-1555
WALT DISNEY RESORTS	☎ 800-647-7900
WYNDHAM HOTELS	☎ 800-822-4200

FINDING THE LOCATION OF THE ADDRESS

Big Apple Street Smarts: Manhattan, for the most part, is a grid. Using the chart below you can come extremely close in calculating the nearest cross street or avenue to your destination. You stand a better chance of a correct answer than if you ask a stranger for directions.

Use this guide to find any address in the Big Apple quickly and easily. Simply drop the final digit from the building number. Then divide the remaining figure in half and add or subtract the number indicated below. The result will be the number of the nearest cross-street.

Avenues A.B C D	+3	Eighth Avenue	+9
First Avenue	+3	Ninth & Tenth	+13
Second	+3	Eleventh	+15
Third	+10	Amsterdam	+59
Fourth	+8	Columbus	+59
Fifth		Lexington	+22
1-200	+13	Madison	+27
201-400	+16	Park	+34
401-600	+18	West End	+59
601-775	+20	Central Park West	*
776-1286	*	Riverside Drive	*
Avenue of the Americas		Broadway	
(Sixth)	-12	1-754	Below 8th St.
Seventh		754-858	-29
1-1800	+12	859-958	-25
1801 +	+20	1000 +	-31

*Exceptions: Compute in same fashion without dividing in half:

Fifth Avenue		Riverside Drive	
776-1286	-18	1-567	+73
Central Park West	+60	567+	+78

For example to find the nearest cross street for 1515 Broadway: Drop final digit, i.e. 5. Take the 151 and divide by 2 = 75. Subtract 31 = 44th St.

Nearest Avenues on east-west streets are determined as follows:

EAST SIDE		WEST SIDE	
1	Fifth Avenue	1	Fifth Avenue
101	Park Avenue	101	Sixth Avenue
201	Third Avenue	201	Seventh Avenue
301	Second Avenue	301	Eighth Avenue
401	First Avenue	401	Ninth Avenue
501	York or Avenue A	501	Tenth Avenue
601	Avenue B	601	Eleventh Avenue

FREE IN THE BIG APPLE

*Big Apple Street Smarts: Weather permitting there are mimes, magicians, musicians, and jugglers performing all days in front of the **Metropolitan Museum of Art**, 82nd Street and Fifth Avenue and at the **South Street Seaport**, East River at Fulton Street. During the winter, the skaters at Rockefeller Plaza, can provide hours of free entertainment.*

Beware of stopping to watch the sharks who play 3 card monte throughout the city. Shills win. You won't! Even if you don't play, you may lose your wallet to pickpockets who work the crowd.

Most museums, except those listed below, require an admission fee or strongly request a donation. Some have free days or free evenings. It is worth a phone call to verify current policy. A family of four can run up a substantial tab visiting the Big Apple's many museums.

Verify hours and location. Even museums move! Central Park won't!

African American Institute, 833 United Nations Plaza. Hours Mon-Fri 8:30am-5:30pm. Closed weekend and major holidays. Changing African exhibits. ☎ 949-5666

Afro Arts Cultural Center, 2191 Adam Clayton Powell Jr. Blvd. and West 130 St. Hours: Mon.-Sat. 9am-6pm. Contains exhibits of African artifacts, historical and religious items. ☎ 831-3922

American Numismatic Society, 155th St. and Broadway. Hours: Tues-Sat 9-4:30; Sun 1-4. International exhibits of money including many rare items. ☎ 234-3130

American Stock Exchange, 86 Trinity Pl. Hours: Mon-Fri 10-3:30. Closed on most holidays. Guided tour of the exchange, exhibits, observation balcony. ☎ 306-1000

Aunt Len's Doll and Toy Museum, 6 Hamilton Terrace near West 144th St. and Convent Ave. 3000 antique and modern dolls on exhibit, complete with dial and furnishings, doll accessories. By appointment only. ☎ 281-4143

Bible House, 1865 Broadway. Hours: Mon-Fri. 9am-5pm. Rare bibles, fragments of the Dead Sea Scrolls, other religious artifacts on display. ☎ 408-1200

Cathedral of St. John the Divine, 1047 Amsterdam Ave. Hours: Daily 7-5. Tours Mon-Sat 11, 2; Sun 12:30. Begun in 1892, it is still being completed. It is the largest Gothic structure in the world. Its organ contains 70,000 pipes; exceptional stained-glass windows, Biblical Garden. Tours available. ☎ 316-7400

Castle Clinton National Monument, in Battery Park. Hours Memorial Day - Labor Day, daily 9-5. Rest of year, Mon-Fri 9-5. Built in 1811, the fort contains historical exhibits. ☎ 344-7220

Central Park, 59th-110th Sts. between 5th Ave. and Central Park West. Hours: Daily - Avoid after sunset unless there is a concert or special event attracting a crowd. Free summer concerts. 840 acres of landscaped grounds and lakes in the center of the Big Apple.

Chinese Museum, 8 Mott St. Hours: Daily 10am-midnight. Contains cultural and historical exhibits dating back to ancient China. ☎ 964-1542

Energy Museum, Con Edison, 145 E. 14th St. Hours: Tues-Sat 10-4. Closed Sun. History of energy presented through exhibits. Also exhibits on Thomas Edison and his contributions to electricity. ☎ 460-6244

Federal Hall National Memorial, corner of Wall St. & Nassau St. Hours: Memorial Day-Labor Day, daily 9-5; rest of year, Mon-Fri 9-5. Present structure built 1842. First used as a U.S. Customs House, then the U.S. Subtreasury Building. Displays and audio-visual exhibits of historical importance ☎ 264-8701

Federal Reserve Bank of New York, 33 Liberty St. Hours: Tours Mon-Fri 10-2, by appointment. Guided tour offered by reservation. ☎ 720-5000

Fire Department Museum, 278 Spring St. Hours: Tues.-Sat. 10am-4pm. Authentic 19th and 20th century fire fighting apparatus and equipment. Displays of famous fires. ☎ 691-1303

General Grant National Memorial, Riverside Dr. & W. 122nd St. Hours: Memorial Day-Labor Day, daily 9-5. Rest of year, Wed-Sun 9-5. ☎666-1640

Grand Central Station, 42nd St. between Lexington and Vanderbilt Aves. Hours: Daily 24 hours. Tours Wed. 12:30 ☎ 935-3960

Hispanic Society of America, Broadway between 155 & 156th St. Hours: Tues.-Sat. 10am-4:30pm, Sun. 1-4. Closed Mon. Spanish and Portuguese art exhibits. ☎ 926-2234

Info-Quest Center, 550 Madison Ave. Operated by AT&T. Open daily except Mon. 9am-6pm, Tues 10am -9pm. Tour the world of computers, software, fiber optics, lightwave communications. Multimedia presentation.

International Business Machines, 590 Madison Ave. Hours: Tues-Fri 10am-4pm. Closed Sat.-Mon. Exhibit center with changing displays. ☎ 745-6100

Japan House, 333 E. 47th St. Hours: Daily 11am-5pm. Traditional and contemporary Japanese art exhibits. ☎ 832-1155

New York Stock Exchange, 30 Broad St. Hours: Mon-Fri 10am-3:30pm. Tours of the exchange; visitors gallery. ☎ 809-7170

Police Academy of the New York City Police Department, 235 E. 20th St. Hours: Mon-Fri 9-5. Guided tours: a jail, police precinct, firearms range, exhibits of police history, narcotics display. ☎ 477-9753

Saint Mark's In-The-Bowery Church, 2nd Avenue & 10th St. Hours: Mon-Fri 9:30am-5pm. Built in 1795. Peter Stuyvesant is buried here. ☎ 673-9402

St. Paul's Chapel, 11 Vesey St. Hours: Daily 7am-4pm. Dedicated 1766, the oldest standing church in Manhattan. ☎ 732- 5564

Saint Patrick's Cathedral, Fifth Ave. & 50th St. Hours: Daily 7 a.m.- 8 p.m. ☎ 753-2261

Schapiro's Winery, 126 Rivington St. Hours: Tours Sun. 11am-4pm; Mon.-Fri. by appointment. Grapes brought from upstate New York are fermented and aged here. ☎ 674-4404

Seagram Building Tour, 375 Park Ave. Hours: Tues at 3. Tour includes an antique glass display. ☎ 572-7000

Songwriters Hall of Fame, 873 Third Ave. Hours: Mon-Sat 11-3. Closed Sun. Exhibits relating to famous songwriters. ☎ 319-1444

Temple Emanuel, Fifth Ave. at 65th St. Hours: Sun.-Fri. holidays, 10am-5pm. One of the largest Jewish houses of worship in the world. ☎774-1400

Trinity Church, 74 Trinity Place. Hours:Mon-Fri 8-6; Sat.-Sun., holidays 8-4. Built 1696-7. Robert Fulton and Alexander Hamilton are buried here. ☎ 602-0800

United Nations General Assembly Meetings, 46th St. & First Ave. Hours: Mon-Fri 10:30 and 3. Free tickets to sit in on the General Assembly meetings available on a first come, first served basis. ☎ 697-3232

THE CITY NEVER SLEEPS

Big Apple Street Smarts: Areas of the Big Apple that are safe during daylight hours are often deserted and less safe at 3am. If you make a trip to an all night restaurant or pharmacy, it would be wise to take a cab or not travel alone.

Open 24 hours or almost 24 hours.

Pharmacies ● Drug Stores

Kaufman Pharmacy
Lexington Ave. at 50th   ☎ 755-2266

Love Discount
2030 Broadway   ☎ 877-4141

Manhattan Love
2181 Broadway   ☎ 595-7711

Medical Emergency Rooms

Big Apple Street Smarts: All emergency rooms are not equal. You can request that Emergency Services ambulances take you to the hospital with which your doctor is affiliated, but it's up to the EMS crew to make the call. If you can manage to get to the hospital without EMS, you can choose the hospital. Remember that EMS personnel are trained paramedics. They may save your life! But, when the mayor was ill, he didn't go to a city run hospital! Our picks follow.

The address provided is the location of the Emergency Room Entrance:

Beth Israel Medical Center
First Ave. & 16th St.

Lenox Hill Hospital
100 East 77th St.

Mount Sinai Medical Center
Madison & 99th St.

New York Downtown Hospital
170 William St.

New York Hospital-Cornell Medical Center
525 East 68th St.

St. Luke's-Roosevelt Hospital
428 West 59th St.

St. Vincent's Hospital
153 West 11th St.

Doctors Who Make Housecalls

*Big Apple Street Smarts: These numbers reach a service
which will dispatch a doctor to make a house call.*

Doctor's on Call   ☎ 737-2333

New York Medical   ☎ 652-5858

Dentists

All City Emergency Services
230 Park Ave.   ☎ 286-0716

Preventive Dental Associates
200 Madison Ave.   ☎ 683-2568

Billiards

Chelsea Billiards   ☎ 989-0096
54 West 21st St.

Restaurants ● Bistros ● Diners

Angelo's Pizza & Deli
684 Third Ave.   ☎ 687-5151

Around the Clock
8 Stuyvesant St.   ☎ 598-0402

Astoria Rivera
454 Lafayette St.   ☎ 677-4461

Brasserie
100 East 53rd St.   ☎ 751-4840

Carnegie Deli (until 4am)
854 Seventh Ave.   ☎ 757-2245

Charlie's Pizza
140 East 58th St.   ☎ 421-5469

The Green Kitchen
1477 First Ave. ☎ 988-4163

Empire Diner
210 Tenth Ave. ☎ 243-2736

Florent
69 Gansevoort St. ☎ 989-5779

H & H Bagels
2239 Broadway ☎ 595-8000

Kiev Restaurant
117 Second Ave. ☎ 674-4040

Michael's Restaurant Cafe
1733 First Ave. ☎ 410-3600

New York Delicatessen
104 West 57th St. ☎ 541-8320

Newsstands

1st Ave. and 63rd, 65th and 69th St.

2nd Ave. & 53rd and 61st St.

3rd Ave. & 54th St.

Broadway & 72nd, 79th and 94th St.

Lexington Ave. & 57th, 64th and 86th St.

Copy Centers

Kinko's
24 E. 12th St. ☎ 924-0802

Kinko's
2872 Broadway ☎ 316-3390

SMP - Stats - Blowups
26 East 22nd St. ☎ 254-2282

Towing

Big Apple Auto Repair
236 West 50th St. ☎ 315-2518

JDS Towing
602 West 47th St. ☎ 947-2749

Jimmy's Towing Service
640 West 43rd St. ☎ 489-6718

Car Rentals

Avis
217 East 43rd St. ☎ 800-331-1212

Hertz
310 East 48th St. ☎ 800-654-3131

National
305 East 80th St. ☎ 535-1089

Gas Stations

Absolute Auto
326 Bowery ☎ 674-2827

Amoco
7th Ave. at 20th St. ☎ 255-9611

Gulf
6th Ave. at 17th St. ☎ 255-1492

Mobil
11th Ave. at 57th St. ☎ 582-9269

Electricians

AA Electric Co.
40 West 77th St. ☎ 877-7122

Marty Allen Electrical Co.
920 Broadway ☎ 254-9600

Irwin Electrical Co., Inc.
165 West 46th St. ☎ 840-6288

Plumbers

ABAC Contracting Co.
139 West 28th St. ☎ 473-2024

Brill & Brill, Inc.
303 East 11th St.   ☎ 876-8730

Locksmiths

Central Park West Locksmith
1529 Third Ave.   ☎ 410-1607

Champion Locksmiths
340 East 73rd St.   ☎ 362-7000

Eagle Master Locksmiths
307 3rd Ave.   ☎ 532-1075

Eagle Locksmiths
2449A Broadway   ☎ 877-7787

Murray Hill Security Center
444 3rd Ave.   ☎ 532-1652

Night & Day Locksmith
1335 Lexington Ave.   ☎ 722-1017

Rainbow Locksmith Co.
1713 2nd Ave.   ☎ 860-2219

Speedy Locksmiths
21 1st Ave.   ☎ 475-6840

Star Locksmith
238 East 58th St.   ☎ 734-0744

Animal Hospitals

East Side Animal Hospital
321 East 52nd St.   ☎ 751-5176

Park East Animal Hosiptal
52 East 64th St.   ☎ 832-8417

Art Galleries

Around the Clock Cafe
8 Stuyvesant St.   ☎ 598-0402

Beauty Parlors/Barbers

Astor Place Hair
2 Astor Place   ☎ 475-9854

Larry Matthew's Beauty Shop
536 Madison ☎ 355-1900

Car Washes

Carz-A-Poppin
614 Broadway ☎ 673-5115

East Side Brushless Car Wash
1770 First Ave. ☎ 722-2222

West Side Highway Car Wash
638 West 47th St. ☎ 757-1141

Messenger Services

Able Motorized Delivery ☎ 687-5515

Bullit Courier ☎ 983-7400

De Santis ☎ 279-3669

Noonlite ☎ 473-2246

Movers

AVI ☎ 391-6727

Meyers ☎ 505-6640

Moishe's Moving ☎ 439-9191

Private Investigators

APB Investigations Inc. ☎ 321-2200

Mutual ☎ 517-8322

Record Stores/Shops

Bleecker Bob's Golden Oldies (noon-1am.)
118 West 3rd St. ☎ 475-9677

Colony Records (10am-midnight)
1619 Broadway ☎ 265-2050

Recording Studios

AAA Recording Studios
130 West 42nd St. ☎ 221-6625

Taxi & Limousine Service

Carmel Car & Limo Service   ☎ 662-2222

Concord Luxury Limousine   ☎ 230-1600

Tel Aviv   ☎ 777-7777

Bars

Big Apple Street Smarts: There are many bars in Manhattan that are open after midnight. Those listed below have been recently recommended as spots for a serious drink. Your hotel concierge will know of others.

If you need a nightcap after midnight.

Ear Inn
326 Spring St. (SoHo)
Hours: Fri.- Sun. 11:30am - 4am   ☎ 226-9060

Milady's Restaurant
160 Prince St. (SoHo)
Hours: Fri. - Sun. 11am - 4am.   ☎ 226-9340

P. J. Carney's
906 Seventh Ave. (57th St.)
Hours: Fri. - Sun. 12pm - 4am   ☎ 664-0056

Peter McManus Cafe
152 Seventh Ave. (19th St.)
Hours: Fri.- Sun. 11am - 3:30am   ☎ 929-9691.

IT'S YOUR CITY HALL!

Big Apple Street Smarts: If you are aware of which buttons to push, City Hall can be remarkably responsive. Don't call the mayor if your problem can be directed to a specific agency. See DROPPING A DIME.

If you are not satisfied with the result or require action at a higher level, try pushing a button at City Hall. Scan the titles and direct phone numbers that follow. There is a good chance that one of them is right on target.

When it is a city agency itself that is the problem, e.g. solicitation of a bribe by a staff member, or an unresponsive reply to a legitimate beef, contact the Inspector General for that agency. The central phone number for the Department of Investigations is listed below. The Inspector General for each agency is independent of the agency! If it is a separate legal entity and not a city agency, e.g. The NYC Transit Authority or The Board Of Education, you will be referred to the appropriate Inspector General.

Office Of The Mayor
City Hall   ☎ 788-3000
New York, N.Y. 10007

First Deputy Mayor   ☎ 788-2999

Deputy Mayor for Public Safety   ☎ 788-6764

Deputy Mayor - Intergovernmental Aff.   ☎ 788-3092

Deputy Mayor - Finance & Development   ☎ 788-3129

Deputy Mayor - Planning & Develop.   ☎ 788-3129

The Mayor's Constituency Offices

African-American/Caribbean Affairs   ☎ 788-2942

Asian Affairs   ☎ 788-2694

European-American Affairs   ☎ 788-2704

Immigrant Affairs   ☎ 566-8930

Latino Affairs   ☎ 788-2720

Office For the Lesbian & Gay Community ☎ 788-2706

Other Special Offices Of The Mayor

Commission on the Status of Women ☎ 788-2738

Mayor's Office Of Transportation ☎ 788-2766

New York City Federal Affairs Office ☎ 788-2641

Office for People with Disabilities ☎ 788-2830

Office of Education Services ☎ 788-6719

Office for Children & Families ☎ 788-6740

Office of State Legislative Affairs ☎ 788-2619

Office of City Legislative Affairs ☎ 788-2920

Office on Health Policy ☎ 788-6700

Office on Homelessness & Single
Room Occupancy Housing Services ☎ 788-2784

Office Of Housing Coordination ☎ 788-2752

Office of Planning & Environmental
Coordination ☎788-2921

Office of Special Projects & Events ☎ 788-2555

NYC Department of Investigations ☎ 825-5900
　　Complaint Line ☎ 825-5959

I'M BOILING MAD - DROPPING THE DIME

Using the phone to make a complaint.

Key to Abbreviations

New York City Agencies
DCA: Department of Consumer Affairs
DEP: Department of Environmental Protection
DOI: Department of Investigations
NYC-DOH: Department of Health
NYC-DOT: Department of Transportation

New York State Agencies
AG: Attorney General
DEC: Department of Environmental Conservation
NYS-DOH: Department of Health
NYS-DOT: Department of Transportation

United States Agencies
US-DOT: Department of Transportation
FAA: Federal Aviation Administration
FTC: Federal Trade Commission

Other Agencies
AUTOCAP: Automotive Consumer Action Program
BBB: Better Business Bureau

Your Complaint Is About

Advertisements
Misleading and deceptive ads:
DCA   ☎ 487-4398
AG   ☎ 416-8345
FTC   ☎ 264-1207

Airlines
Lost luggage, refunds:
DCA   ☎ 487-4398
Delays, overbooking, canceled flights,
and all other service complaints:
US-DOT Office of Intergovernmental
and Consumer Affairs   ☎ 202-336-2220
Safety:
FAA (hotline)   ☎ 800-322-7873
FAA (Eastern Region)   ☎ 718-917-1120
FAA (Washington)   ☎ 202-267-3479

Air Pollution
Carbon monoxide, fumes,
smoke:
DEP   ☎ 966-7500
DEC   ☎ 718-482-4949
Natural-gas odors:
Brooklyn Union Gas   ☎ 718-643-4050
Potentially flammable
substances:
Fire Department   ☎ 911
NYFD Bureau of Fire
Prevention   ☎ 718-403-1416

Ambulances
Slow service, non-response to call,
improper or Inadequate care, conduct:
NYS-DOH,
Emergency Medical Service   ☎ 718-326-0600

Animals, Birds, Insects
Bites:
Animals Affairs Bureau   ☎ 334-2618
Dead on city highway:
NYC-DOT   ☎ 323-8548
Dead on city street:
Department of Sanitation   ☎ 219-8090
Dead on private property:
Department of Sanitation   ☎ 219-8090
Pest control (rats, pigeons,
roaches):
NYC-DOH   ☎ 693-4637
Pet-store purchases get sick
or die:
DCA   ☎ 487-4398
Strays; abused, unlicensed,
or wounded animals:
American Society for the
Prevention of Cruelty
to Animals (ASPCA)   ☎ 876-7700

Automobiles
Abandoned (with plates):
Local police precinct   ☎ 374-4303
Abandoned (without plates):
Department of
Transportation   ☎ 219-8090
Gas-station adulteration,
cheating:
DCA   ☎ 487-4398
Leasing-company disputes:

DCA   ☎ 487-4398
Lemons and warranties
(new car):
BBB (GM cars only)   ☎ 533-6200
AUTOCAP (all other
manufacturers)   ☎ 800-522-3881
New-car-dealers disputes,
service, conduct,
practices, purchases, and
leases:
Audi   ☎ 800-822-2834
BMW   ☎ 201-573-2100
Buick   ☎ 800-521-7300
Cadillac   ☎ 800-458-8006
Chevrolet   ☎ 800-222-1020
Chrysler   ☎ 914-359-0110
Fiat   ☎ 201-393-4042
Ford   ☎ 201-288-9421
Honda   ☎ 609-235-5533
Isuzu   ☎ 201-784-1414
Jaguar   ☎ 201-592-5200
Mazda   ☎ 904-731-4010
Mercedes-Benz   ☎ 201-573-0600
Mitsubishi   ☎ 800-222-0037
Nissan   ☎ 800-647-7261
Oldsmobile   ☎ 517-377-5546
Peugeot   ☎ 800-345-5549
Pontiac   ☎ 800-762-2737
Porsche   ☎ 702-348-3154
Saab   ☎ 800-255-9007
Subaru   ☎ 914-359-2500
Toyota   ☎ 800-331-4331
Volkswagen   ☎ 914-578-5000
Volvo   ☎ 201-767-4737

Rental-agency problems:
DCA   ☎ 487-4398

Towing complaints and rate
disputes (private company):
DCA   ☎ 788-4636

Used-car-odometer tampering
and other used-car-dealer
problems:
DCA   ☎ 487-4398

Unsafe vehicles:
Auto Safety Hotline
of the Federal DOT   ☎ 800-424-9393

Highway
Traffic Safety
Administration ☎ 800-424-9393

Banks
(see "Financial Institutions")

Block Parties, Street Events, Street Fairs
Unsafe amusement rides:
DCA ☎ 487-4398
Ripoffs, interference with
business or residence:
Community Assistance Unit
of Mayor's Office ☎ 566-2506
Late-night noise:
Call this number to find your
Local police precinct ☎ 374-4303

Building Hazards
Malfunctioning elevator
doors, obstructions,
improper lighting, dangerous
stairways, floor hazards:
Department of Buildings ☎ 312-8530

Buses
Lateness, poor service, driver
misconduct, and other complaints:
City buses:
NYC Transit Authority ☎ 718-330-3322
Private bus lines:
NYC Franchise Bureau: for the
sixteen franchised bus lines. ☎ 669-4500

Charter Buses:
NYS-DOT ☎ 718-482-4594

Businesses & Stores
Billing disputes, layaway
problems, defective and
damaged merchandise, flea
markets, going-out-of-
business sales, fire sales,
liquidation sales, ripoffs,
fraud:
DCA ☎ 487-4398
BBB ☎ 533-6200

Cable Television
Billing errors, poor reception,
unsatisfactory repair, slow or
unresponsive service or hookup.

First, call your cable company's
customer service line.
If the dispute remains unresolved,
call the city agency that oversees
cable companies:
NYC Bureau of Franchises   ☎ 788-6540

Cigarette Smoke
Violations and non-enforcement
of no-smoking ordinances:
NYC-DOH Smoking
Enforcement Unit   ☎ 693-4637

City Hall Government Agencies
Corruption: general and
individual, unethical
practices, poor service,
and other disputes:
NYC Department of
Investigation (DOI)   ☎ 825-5959
City Council-Ombudsman   ☎ 669-7635
NYS Investigation
Commission   ☎ 577-0700
NYS Special Prosecutor   ☎ 815-0400

Contracts
Fraud, cancellation, and
other disputes:
DCA   ☎ 487-4398

Credit Bureaus
Refusal to correct errors on
Credit Report: FTC   ☎ 264-1220

Dating Services
Complaints:
DCA   ☎ 487-4398

Day Camps
Personnel misconduct, unsafe
conditions, and other
problems:
Bureau of Day Camps and
Recreation   ☎ 566-7763

**Day Care, Pre-kindergarten
and Nursery Schools**
Unsafe or unhealthy
conditions, unlicensed

facilities, misconduct:
NYC-DOH   ☎ 334-7803

Dentists
(see "Licensed Professionals")

Department Stores
Delivery foul-ups; billing
errors and disputes; sale
items not available;
damaged, nonworking, or
incomplete merchandise;
other complaints
B = billing problems
FD = furniture-delivery problems
CS = customer-service complaints
M = main switchboard, ask for
customer service
EXT = extension number):

A & S	☎ (M) 718-875-7200 ☎
	(B) EXT 4600
Barneys New York	☎ (M) 929-9000
	☎ (CS) EXT 363
Bergdorf Goodman	☎ (CS) 872-8871
Bloomingdale's	☎ (CS) 355-5900
Lord & Taylor	☎ (M) 391-3344
Macy's	☎ (CS, B) 736-5151 ☎
	(FD) 800-526-1202
Saks Fifth Avenue	☎ (B) 940-5555
	☎ (M) 753-4000 ☎
	(CS) EXT 2845

Unresolved disputes:
DCA   ☎ 487-4398

Diplomats, United Nations
*Big Apple Street Smarts: Don't give
credit, enter into leases or other
contracts to diplomats without obtaining
a written waiver of diplomatic immunity.*

Illegal parking, accident damage
from diplomat's car, landlord-tenant
problems, and other complaints
about undiplomatic relations:
NYC Commission for the United Nations
and for the Consular Corps   ☎ 319-9300

Discrimination
Employment:
NYC Commission on
Human Rights Intake   ☎ 788-4636

NYS Division of Human
Rights ☎ 870-8400
US Equal Employment
Commission ☎ 264-7161
US Department of Health
and Human Services, Civil
Rights ☎ 264-3313
Housing:
NYC Commission on Human
Rights, Fair Housing ☎ 306-7500
NYS Division of Human
Rights ☎ 870-8400

Doctors
Misconduct, unnecessary
procedures, referrals for
billing disputes:
NYS-DOH's Professional
Medical Conduct Division ☎ 613-2650

Drugs (illegal)
Presence of drug-dealers:
Call this number to find your
local precinct phone
number ☎ 374-4303
NYPD Narcotics
Complaints ☎ 374-6620

Dry Cleaning & Laundromats
Damaged or lost items,
poor-quality cleaning,
and other complaints:
DCA ☎ 487-4398
Neighborhood Cleaners
Association ☎ 684-0945

Electric Utility-Con Ed
Billing disputes, service
cutoff, and other complaints:
Con Ed - call customer-service number
on your bill.
NYS Public Service
Commission ☎ 219-3550
Improper repair after tearing
up street or sidewalk:
NYC-DOT ☎ 964-2110

Financial Institutions
Banks, Check-cashing
establishments, Credit

Unions, Finance Companies,
Loan Companies, S & Ls,
Automated-teller-machine
problems, credit-card-billing
errors, disputed bills,
improper practices, credit
discrimination, and other
complaints:
Federal Reserve State
Member Banks:
Federal Reserve Board,
Division of Consumer and
Community Affairs ☎ 201-452-3946
National Banks:
Comptroller of the Currency,
Northeastern District ☎ 819-9860
Federal S & Ls:
Federal Home Loan Bank
Board ☎ 202-906-6237
Federal Credit Unions:
National Credit Union
Administration. ☎ 518-472-4554
State-chartered banks and
credit unions, finance
companies, loan companies,
check-cashing services,
incorrect savings-rate
and yield quotes:
NYS Banking Department ☎ 618-6445
Insufficient loan disclosure,
misstated APR interest rates,
and other federal
Truth-in-Lending-law
violations:
FTC ☎ 264-1207
DCA ☎ 487-4398

Food
Food sold in supermarkets
that is adulterated, rotten,
unwholesome, or otherwise
unfit for consumption,
deceptively designated
kosher, or improperly graded:
NYS Department of
Agriculture and Markets ☎ 718-260-2877
Meat and poultry problems:
US Department of
Agriculture Hotline ☎ 800-535-4555
Misdated milk and
complaints about
delis, take-out food,

restaurants, and bakeries:
NYC-DOH ☎ 693-4637
Complaints about food at
farmer's markets and food
co-ops:
NYS Department of
Agriculture and Markets ☎ 718-260-2877
Unsanitary conditions:
NYC-DOH ☎ 285-9503
Short-weighted food,
unit-pricing-law
violations, sale items
not available, undated
perishables e.g. bread,
cheese, eggs:
DCA ☎ 487-4398
Tampering, poisoning:
FDA Inspector General's
Hotline ☎ 800-368-5779
FBI ☎ 335-2700

Funerals
Pricing problems, not
providing service
agreed to, providing and
charging for services not
contracted for, hidden fees,
and other problems:
DCA ☎ 487-4398
NYS-DOH ☎ 518-453-1989

Furniture & Home Furnishings
Misdelivery/late delivery, billing
errors, damaged merchandise:
DCA ☎ 487-4398

Garbage
Non-pickup on public streets and other
complaints:
NYC Sanitation
Department ☎ 219-8090

Guns
To report a person with a gun, call
this number which is a toll free
hotline established by the Federal
Bureau of Alcohol, Tobacco and Fire
Arms and the New York City Police
Department. ☎ 1-800-ATF-Guns

45

Home-Improvement Contractors

Ripoffs, shoddy workmanship, not
performing work agreed to, overcharging,
absconding with down payment, damages
to property:
DCA ☎ 487-4398

Hospitals

Slow emergency-room service, billing
errors, improper care, and other complaints:
City-owned hospitals:
NYC Health and Hospitals
Corporation ☎ 566-8086
Private and other hospitals:
NYS-DOH, Hospital Unit ☎ 502-0855

Housing

Service cutoffs, non-repair, unsafe
conditions, housing-code violations,
landlord problems, e.g. no heat, no
smoke detectors.
All public and private housing, City-owned
co-ops:
NYC Department of Housing
Preservation and
Development ☎ 960-4800
State-owned co-ops:
NYS Division of Rent
Administration ☎ 718-739-6400
Lofts:
NYC Loft Board ☎ 566-1438
Window guards:
NYC-DOH ☎ 693-4637
Rent control and
Stabilization:
NYS Division of Housing
and Community
Renewal Hotline ☎ 718-739-6400
Problems with condominium
and co-op conversions:
NYS Attorney General -
Real Estate Finance Bureau ☎ 416-8121
Disputes over interest on
rent security deposit:
NYS Consumer Fraud
and Protection Bureau ☎ 416-8345

Insurance

Non-payment of valid claim, premium
and billing errors, unwarranted
cancellation of coverage, and other
disputes:

NYS Department of
Insurance   ☎ 602-0203

Lawyers
Conflict of interest, overbilling,
unethical conduct, poor service:
Disciplinary Committee   ☎ 685-1000

Licensed Professionals
Ripoffs, shoddy work, damages, conflict
of interest, unethical conduct, and
other complaints (but not billing disputes):
Accountants, architects, chiropractors,
dentists, masseurs, nurses, opticians,
optometrists, physical therapists,
psychologists.:
NYS Education Department's Office
of Professional Discipline   ☎ 951-6400
Barbers, beauticians, cosmetologists,
hairdressers, notaries, private
investigators:
NYS Department of State's
Division of Licensing   ☎ 417-5747
Electricians:
Bureau of Electrical Control ☎ 669-8353
Engineers, pharmacists:
NYS Education Department's Office
of Professional Discipline   ☎ 951-6400
Plumbers:
NYC Department of
Buildings   ☎ 791-1710

Mail
Mail fraud, obscene mail,
theft, service complaints:
US Postal Inspector   ☎ 330-3844
Mail-ordered item never
delivered:
DCA   ☎ 487-4398
Mail-Order Action Line of the
Direct Mail Marketing
Association   ☎ 768-7277
Late delivery and non-
delivery, poor window
service, damaged mail:
Postmaster, New York   ☎ 330-3668
US Postal Service
Consumer Advocate☎   ☎ 202-268-2284
To stop Unwanted
Commercial Mail:

Direct Mail Marketing
Association   ☎ 768-7277

Motion Picture and Television Production
Interference with business or residence,
improper conduct of production and
security personnel, damages to property,
unsafe conditions, injuries due to equipment:
Mayor's Office of Film,
Theater and Broadcasting   ☎ 489-6710

Moving & Storage
Overcharging, late delivery, damage,
low-ball estimates/hidden charges,
weight bumping, and other moving-company
complaints:
DCA   ☎ 487-4398
Interstate:
US Interstate Commerce
Commission   ☎ 264-1072
Storage-company problems:
DCA   ☎ 487-4398

Natural Gas
Con-Ed
billing disputes, service cutoff,
and other complaints:
Con Ed: Phone Number On Your Bill
NYS Public Service
Commission   ☎ 219-3550

Noise Pollution
Loud neighbors, noisy parties, car
alarms, crowds or groups outside window:
NYC Police Department (for
the phone-number of your
local precinct)   ☎ 374-4303
DCA Quality of Life
Night Squad   ☎ 487-4398
Aircraft noise:
FAA   ☎ 718-917-1022
General noise pollution
from construction, air
conditioners, and other
sources:
NYC Department of
Environmental Protection   ☎ 966-7500

Nursing Homes
Mistreatment of residents,
unsafe or unsanitary

conditions:
NYS-DOH   ☎ 502-0874
Not providing services, and
other Medical Fraud:
AG Medicaid Fraud
Control Unit   ☎ 587-5300

Parking Lots and Garages
Overcharging, damage to vehicle,
missing or stolen items, improper
price disclosure, and other complaints:
DCA   ☎ 487-4398

Parking Meters
Broken, malfunctions
NYC Traffic Department   ☎ 718-830-7632

Pharmacists
Improper practices, overcharging,
misstating availability of generic
drugs, and other complaints:
NYS Department of Education's Office
of Professional Discipline ☎ 951-6400
NYS Department of Education,
Board of Pharmacy   ☎ 951-6400

Playgrounds
Park and playground hazards,
damaged equipment, repairs
needed, downed tree limbs,
and other problems:
NYC Department of Parks
and Recreation☎   ☎ 800-834-3823

Police Misconduct
Rights violations, other
complaints:
Civilian Review Board   ☎ 323-8750

Potholes
NYC-DOT   ☎ 964-2100

Psychiatrists
Misconduct, billing disputes:
NYS-DOH's Professional
Medical Conduct Division   ☎ 340-3363

Real Estate Brokers & Salespeople
Unethical conduct, commission disputes,
conflict of interest, contract breaches,

and other complaints:
NYS Department of State's
Division of Licensing ☎ 417-5747

Repairmen
Non-repair of item, overcharging or
hidden charges, damage, lost item:
DCA ☎ 487-4398

Restaurants
Unsanitary Conditions:
NYC-DOH ☎ 693-4637

Schools
Student suspension, incompetent teacher,
student-teacher conflicts, teacher
misconduct, grade and course-credit
disputes:
Private and Parochial schools
(elementary grades through high school)
and other non-public schools:
NYS Department of
Education ☎ 518-474-3879
Public Schools:
NYC Board of Education ☎ 718-933-2000
Fast-buck operations, fraud,
refunds, and contract
disputes, involving private
vocational, correspondence,
business, trade, and
technical schools:
NYS Department of
Education ☎ 488-3252

Sewers
Backed-up, nonfunctioning, or blocked
storm drains; odors; other complaints:
NYC Environmental Protection
Communications Center ☎ 966-7500

Sidewalks
Illegal sidewalk cafes:
DCA ☎ 487-4398
Cracked sidewalks, holes,
improper repair after public-
utility work - DOT ☎ 323-8548
NYC Department of Highways,
Sidewalk Division ☎ 323-8501
Scaffolding and rigging
obstructing sidewalk in
unsafe manner; careless
scaffold workers:

NYC Department of
Buildings   ☎ 312-8312

Stockbrokers
Unethical practices, account disputes,
unauthorized sales or purchases, fraud,
hidden fees, excessive commissions:
US Securities and Exchange
Commission   ☎ 264-1620

Street Cleaning
NYC Department of
Sanitation   ☎ 219-8090

Street Lights
Broken, damaged, unsafe:
NYC-DOT   ☎ 566-2525
Bureau of Traffic   ☎ 669-8312

Street Peddlers & Sidewalk Stands
Non-food peddler ripoffs, food-peddler
short-weighing and problems with fruit,
vegetable, soft drink, tobacco, flowers,
ice cream, candy, and bootblack sidewalk
stands:
DCA   ☎ 487-4398
Sidewalk stands other than those listed
above taking up excessive sidewalk space:
NYC Department of
Highways   ☎ 566-5792
Food peddlers, unsanitary conditions:
NYC-DOH   ☎ 285-9503
Any peddler obstructing street or
sidewalk traffic, annoying other
business customers, and other problems:
NYC Police Department (for the phone #
of your local precinct)   ☎ 374-4303

Streetwalkers
Soliciting:
NYC Police Department (for the phone #-
of your local precinct)   ☎ 374-4303

Subways
Late or delayed trains, improper
personnel conduct, unsafe platforms
or trains, and other complaints:
NYC Transit Authority   ☎ 718-330-3322

Tax Preparers
Misconduct, billing disputes, poor
service, misrepresentations:
DCA ☎ 487-4398

Taxis
Overcharging, injuries, damage to
property, meter cheating, refusal
to take customer to certain
destinations, and other misconduct:
NYC Taxi and Limousine
Commission ☎ 221-TAXI

Telephones
Bad connections, billing errors,
installation or service delays,
equipment problems, charges for calls
you didn't make:
New York Telephone
(complaints unresolved after
you've called your
business-office phone #
number, which appears on
your bill. ☎ 800-722-2300
AT&T ☎ 800-222-0300
MCI ☎ 800-444-3333
Sprint ☎ 800-877-4646
Unresolved disputes with
any phone company:
NYS Public Service
Commission ☎ 488-5330

Obscene Phone Calls: ☎ 800-522-1122

Tickets
Refunds for canceled events,
abbreviated performances, and
other ticketing problems at movie
theaters, stage productions,
sports events, and live performances:
DCA ☎ 487-4398

Traffic
Lights and signs damaged, unsafe:
NYC-DOT ☎ 566-2525

Travel Agencies
Botched reservations, overcharging,
hidden charges, misrepresentations,
refunds:
DCA ☎ 487-4398

Litter and illegal dumping:
NYC Department of
Sanitation ☎ 219-8090

Voting
Election-law violations, registration
foul-ups, electioneering in polling
place, intimidation, vote fraud:
NYC Board of Elections ☎ 924-1860
NYS Board of Elections ☎ 587-4825

Water
Water-quality problems:
NYC-DOH ☎ 693-4637
Pollution, low pressure:
NYC Environmental Protection
Communication Center ☎ 966-7500

Workplace
Poor workplace conditions and other
labor complaints:
NYS Department of Labor/Division of
Labor Standards ☎ 718-797-7499

Wage-related disputes:
US Department of Labor,
Wage and Hour Division ☎ 264-8185
Individual contract disputes with
union, union voting problems, union
pension-plan problems, and other
disputes between union members and
unions:
US Department of Labor,
Labor Management
Standards ☎ 377-2580
National Labor Relations
Board ☎ 264-0300
Unsafe conditions:
US Occupational Safety
and Health Administration ☎ 337-2356

HELP FROM HOTLINES

Advice and help for yourself, friends, and family is available from a variety of Hotlines. The majority are free. Many of the hotlines below are unlisted. The majority are 24 hour hotlines.

Big Apple Street Smarts: Information lines that have phone numbers beginning with 540, 900 cost $$$!

Crisis Lines

Alcoholism	☎ 1-800-252-2557
Child Abuse	☎ 1-800-342-3720
Crime In Progress	☎ 911
Domestic Violence	☎ 1-800-942-6908
Drug Abuse	☎ 1-800-522-5353
Fire In Progress	☎ 911
Medical Emergency	☎ 911
National AIDS Hotline	☎ 1-800-234-2437
Runaways	☎ 619-6884
Sex Crimes	☎ 267-7273
Victims Services	☎ 577-7777

Crime Victims Board

If you are a victim of a crime that takes place in the Big Apple, you may be compensated by the New York State Crime Victims Board. Report the crime to the police and obtain a number for your case. Then call the board at ☎ 587-5160 and they will send you a form to complete. Keep a copy and send it to the address in Albany that is set forth on the form.

Miscellaneous

Better Business Bureau   ☎ 900-463-6222
Hours: 24 hours
Information on companies and charities. Touch tone phone required. Be prepared with company or charity phone number and zip code. 95¢ per minute with average call costing $3.80. From 8:30am to 8pm, you can call from any phone and use a credit card. Information is free if you write.

Bureau of Labor Statistics Hot Lines
Hours: All three below are 24-hour recorded message numbers.
Consumer Price Index: ☎-337-2405
Unemployment Statistics: ☎-337-2410
Weekly BLS Research Findings: ☎-337-2411

Federal Information Center
Service: Call if you have a question for some government agency but you are not sure which one or for affairs of the nation. ☎ 800-347-1977

Graffiti Hotline ☎ 427-6100
Hours: Staffed 24 hours
Service: This service will clean up graffiti, and complaints will also be taken.

Sky Reporter ☎ 769-5917
Service: The Hayden Planetarium's 24-hour night-sky information line provides amateur astronomers with updates on moon phases and the locations of stars and planets.

Sleep Line ☎ 439-2992
Hours: 24 hour recorded message
Service: This service gives you hypnotic repetitions that are likely to put you to sleep right on the spot.

Stop Smoking Line ☎ 439-2990
Hours: 24 hours
Service: Helps smokers to kick the habit.

Subway/Bus Information Line ☎ 718-330-1234
Hours: 24 hour service
Service: This service gives the best destination routes if you are traveling with the Transit Authority.

Tax Help (NYC Tax Assistance) ☎ 718-935-6736
Hours: 24 hour
Service: Recorded tax information.

Tax Evasion Hot Line ☎ 718-403-4310
Hours: Mon-Fri 8:30am-5:30pm
Service: This service accepts callers who wish to report someone whom they suspect of tax evasion. Callers will remain anonymous.

The Plant Hotline ☎ 220-8681
Hours: Mon-Fri 10am-3pm
Service: Connects you with a horticulturist at the New York Botanical Gardens, who will answer all your indoor and outdoor plant questions.

The Union Catalog ☎ 340-0822
Hours: Mon-Sat 9am-5:20pm

Service: This service locates books at Public Libraries. Give them the book's title and author's name.

The Homework Hotline   ☎ 718-780-7766
Hours: Mon.-Thu. 5pm-8pm
Service: Brooklyn Public Library service for students in grades kindergarten through 12th grade.

Vaccination Info. For Travel   ☎ 349-2664
Hours: Mon-Fri 9am-5pm
Service: This service from the Department of Health connects prospective travelers to an operator who will tell them if they need a shot(s) to go to certain places. They will not tell you specifically which shot(s), but they will mail the information to you.

57

Zip Code Hot Line   ☎ 967-8585
Hours: Mon-Fri 8am-8pm
Service: Call this postal service line to get zip codes for any address in the country.

BIG APPLE SOUVENIRS

Big Apple Street Smarts: Souvenirs are sold at smoke shops, a myriad of stores in the Times Square Area, at most museums, in Woolworths, and even some of the department stores. They vary in price and quality. If you are visiting and desirous of taking a souvenir home or a Manhattanite about to visit the outer provinces and need a gift, try CityBooks run by the City for unusual items. Call to verify hours.

CityBooks Store   ☎ 669-8245
61 Chambers St.

CityBooks Store   ☎ 669-8245
2223 Municipal Bldg.
New York, N.Y.10007

A mail order catalog is available. Call or write to the Municipal Building location.

Among our favorites are: The Subway Token Ties, Police and Fire Department Caps and Sweatshirts, Parks Department Sweatshirts, Sanitation Department Sweatshirts, the Big Apple Paperweight and the Official City Seal Mug.

● ● ●

HALF-PRICE THEATER TICKETS

Big Apple Street Smarts: If you don't have your heart set on a particular play and have some time, waiting on line at TKTS saves you half the price of a ticket purchased at the box office. The number of shows offered diminishes as the allotment is sold. Get there early and bring a book or magazine to read. An hour before show time, an unexpected block of tickets may arrive for a popular show that didn't sell out on that day.

On the day of the performance, ½ price tickets are available at the TKTS Booth at Broadway & 47th St. and at 2 World Trade Center. For music and dance the booth is on the south side of 42nd Street just east of 6th Ave. Lines start in AM for matinees and early PM for evening performances.

Dry Cleaning-Cleaners 57
245 East 57th St.   ☎ 759-9057
Hours: Mon-Fri 7:30am-6:30pm, Sat 9am-2pm
American Express is accepted.

Dry Cleaning-One Hour Martinizing(Chelsea)
232 Ninth Ave., near 24th St.   ☎ 255-7317
Hours: Mon-Sat 7am-7pm, Sat 7am-5:30pm, Thurs till 8pm
No credit cards.

Dry Cleaning-Sutton Cleaners
1060 First Ave.,   ☎ 755-1617
Hours: Mon-Fri 7am-6:30pm, Sat 8am-4pm
American Express accepted.

Eyeglasses-Cohen Fashion Optical
Call for Manhattan location nearest to you. ☎ 516-358-4100
Hours: Daily 9am-6pm.
Most eyeglasses and contact-lens prescriptions can be
prepared in an hour. AE, CB, MC, V, D, DC are accepted.

Eyeglasses-Pearle Vision Center
10 East 42nd St.   ☎ 986-2150
Other locations 23rd & 5th, 81st & 1st., 96th & Columbus
Hours: Mon.-Fri. 9am-6pm. - Sat. 10am-4pm.
They can fill most prescriptions in an hour. Other one hour
services are available.
AE, MC, V are accepted.

Eyeglasses-Sarkis Jewelry
578 Fifth Ave.   ☎ 997-1148
Hours: Mon-Fri 10am-5:30pm
Fix broken eyeglasses frames.
No credit cards.

Eyeglasses-Triangle Optical
95 Delancey St.,   ☎ 674-3748
Hours: Mon-Fri 9:30am-5:30pm, Sun 9am-5pm
Offers one hour service on many frames and lenses.
AE, CB, D, DC, MC are accepted.

Photo Developing - Check your neighborhood first. They
proliferate like rabbits.
Photo Developing-Fromex One Hour Photo Systems
150 East 86th St.   ☎ 369-4821
Hours: Mon-Fri 7:30am-7:30pm; S-Sun 10am-7:30pm
They process film in one hour. Several locations.
AE, MC, V are accepted.

Photo Developing-Harvey's 1 Hour Photo
698 Third Ave.   ☎ 682-5045
Hours: Mon-Fri 8am-6pm

61

They process most film in an hour.
AE, MC, V are accepted.

Shoes-A-Rapid Expert Shoe Repair
1322 Third Ave.   ☎ 744-8544
Hours: Mon-Fri 7:30am-7pm, Sat 9am-6pm
They can repair most heels and soles in an hour.
No credit cards.

Shoes-B. Nelson Shoe, Inc.
1221 Sixth Ave.   ☎ 869-3552
Hours: Mon-Fri 7:30am-5:15pm
Some repairs are provided within an hour such as men's heel
replacement, and full-sole replacement.
AE, MC, V are accepted.

Shoes-Eagle Master Shoe and Leather Repair
306 Third Ave.   ☎ 995-2910
Hours: Mon-Fri 7:30am-7pm, Sat 9:30am-5:30pm
Provides some services in one hour.
No credit cards.

Shoes-Manhattan Midtown Shoe Repair
577 Second Ave.   ☎ 684-3906
Hours: Mon-Fri 8am-6:30pm, Sat 9am-5pm
Provides some services in one hour.
No credit cards.

Tailoring-Bhambi's Custom Tailors Ltd.
14 East 60th St.   ☎ 935-5379
Hours: Mon-Fri 10am-7pm, Sat 10am-5pm
Offers various one hour alterations, including adding cuffs to
pants, altering waistlines, altering the seat or crotch, and
adjusting sleeves on jackets.
MC, V are accepted (there is a $50 minimum on credit cards)

Tailoring-Mr. Tony, Inc.
120 West 37th St.   ☎ 594-0930
Hours: Mon-Fri 9am-6:30pm, Sat till 2pm
Provides services such as buttons attached, zippers mended,
and torn pants sewed in one hour.
MC and V are accepted.

Tailoring-Raymond's Tailor Shop
Hours: Mon-Fri 7:30am-6:30pm, Sat 10am-4pm
366 Mott St.   ☎ 226-0747
275 Greenwich St.,   ☎ 962-4185
Many services including alterations done in an hour.
No credit cards.

BABYSITTING SERVICES & DAYCAMPS

Big Apple Street Smarts: Big Apple teenagers often have too large an allowance to motivate them to give up Saturday night. Even if you have a regular babysitter, there will come a time when the flu or some other emergency interferes with your plans. Try one of the agencies, most of which have a four-hour minimum charge. Rates vary depending on whether you request a baby nurse or a baby sitter, the age of the child, and the number of children. Carfare, including cab fare when appropriate, is charged to you.

Avalon Registry ☎ 245-0250
250 West 57th St.

63

Baby Sitters' Guild ☎ 682-0227
60 East 42nd St.

Fox Agency ☎ 753-2686
30 East 60th St.

Gilbert Child Care Agency, Inc. ☎ 757-7900
119 West 57th St.

Sitters On Stand By, Inc. ☎ 838-0134
509 Madison Ave.
New York, NY

Daycamps

Big Apple Street Smarts: A good source for the lowdown on daycamps is the park bench. Talk to parents whose children attended last summer. The better programs fill up quickly. Start your planning in early spring. Unless the camp site is in the neighborhood, the availability of bus or van pickup and delivery programs will be a key factor in whether you and your child will benefit from the camp. While sites outside the city are attractive, be certain that half of your child's day is not spent traveling.

A Dalton Summer
53-61 East 91st St. ☎ 722-5160

Asphalt Green Summer Skills Day Camp
555 East 90th St. ☎ 369-8890

Billdave Summer Day Camp
206 E. 85th St. ☎ 535-7151

Camp Morningside
251 West 100th St. ☎ 316-1555

Corlears Summer Camp
324 West 15th St. ☎ 741-2800

Discovery Programs Summerscene
424 East 89th St. ☎ 348-5371

Family School Summer Day Camp
323 East 47th St. ☎ 688-5950

Kinder Camp at the West Side Y
5 West 63rd St. ☎ 787-4400

Merricats Castle School
Church of the Holy Trinity
316 East 88th St. ☎ 831-1322

Multimedia Preschool Summer Adventure Program
40 Sutton Place ☎ 593-1041

92nd St. YMHA Camps
1395 Lexington ☎ 415-5700

Sutton Gymnastics KinderKamp
440 Lafayette St. ☎ 533-9390

The Little Red School House
196 Bleecker St. ☎ 477-5316

United Nations International School Summer Program
24-50 F.D.R. Drive ☎ 684-7468

AUCTIONS IN THE BIG APPLE

Big Apple Street Smarts: Auctions are among the best free shows in town. They are also educational, particularly if you attend the previews and study the offerings. Call the auction houses to obtain schedules and preview dates. Christie's, Sotheby's, and Swann have very active schedules. The others hold auctions less often. While bargains may be obtained at auction, you should do your homework. Attending the previews and examining the objects that interest you is mandatory if you intend to bid. Don't be afraid to ask the staff questions. Each auction house has its own set of rules as to what, if anything, they guarantee. Read the rules in the auction catalog, if there is one. If there is no catalog, ask for a copy of the bill of sale used by the house; it usually sets forth their policies. Don't wave to friends, the auctioneer may think you are bidding!

Chelsea Auction Associates
38 West 21st Street   ☎ 675-6770

Christie's
502 Park Ave.   ☎ 546-1000

Christie's East
219 East 67th St.   ☎ 606-0400

Greenwich Auction Room Ltd.
110 East 13th St.   ☎ 533-5930

Guernsey's
108½ East 73rd St.   ☎ 794-2280

Lubin Galleries
30 West 26th St.   ☎ 924-3777

Manhattan Galleries
1415 Third Ave.   ☎ 727-0370

Sotheby's
1334 York Ave.   ☎ 606-7000

Swann Galleries
104 East 25th St.   ☎ 254-4710

Tepper Galleries
110 East 25th St.   ☎ 677-5300

William Doyle
175 East 87th St.   ☎ 427-2730

FLEA MARKETS

Big Apple Street Smarts: Paris remains the city that dominates the flea market scene. The Big Apple is not a true contender. It does have several that provide a mix of discounted new merchandise, expensive crafts, and other items which range from junk to authentic antiques. The outdoor markets are by their nature, seasonal. The markets that take place in school yards are often sponsored by the PTA and provide substantial income to augment school activity budgets. From late spring to early fall there are numerous one day street fairs. The variety of merchandise offered ranges from gadgets you also see on late night TV to antique jewelry, books, and prints. The New York Times often lists street fairs for the weekend in its Friday edition.

Battery Park Crafts Exhibit
State St. Promenade between the Bowling Green Subway
Station and Pearl St.　　　☎ 752-8475
Hours: Thurs. 11am-7pm
You will find: crafts and collectibles.

Bryant Park Crafts Show
42nd St. between 5th & 6th　　☎ 752-8475
Hours: Fri 12pm-7pm
You will find: crafts with some antique jewelry.

Canal Street Flea Market
8 Greene St.　　　　　☎ 226-7541
Hours: Sat.-Sun. 10AM-5PM
You will find: hardware to clothing.

Canal West Flea Market
370 Canal St.　　　　　☎ 718-693-8142
Hours: Sat.-Sun. 7am-6pm
You will find: phonograph records to necklaces.

Greenwich Village Flea Market
P.S. 41 Greenwich & Charles　　☎ 752-8475
Hours: Sat 12pm-7pm
You will find: 70 outdoor booths, offering a variety of merchandise.

I.S. 44 Flea Market
Columbus Ave. - 76th & 77th　　☎ 316-1088
Hours: Sun 10am-6pm
You will find: 300 indoor and outdoor vendors, socks to antiques.

P.S. 183 Antique Flea & Farmers Market
East 67th St. bet. 1st & York　　☎ 737-8888
Hours: Sat 6am-6pm
You will find: antique silver-plate to handmade pillows.

The Annex Antiques Fair & Flea Market
Sixth Ave. - 24th to 26th St.   ☎ 243-5343
Hours: Sat-Sun 9am-5pm
You will find: Over 200 vendors, many of which deliver their offerings of collectibles, furniture and other antiques.

Tower Market
Broadway - W.4th & Great Jones   ☎ 718-273-8702
Hours: Sat-Sun 10am-7pm
You will find: mostly new merchandise including shorts, sweatshirts, T-shirts, and earrings.

Walter's Famous Union Square Shoppes
873 Broadway, at 18th St.   ☎ 255-0175
Hours: Tues-Sat 10am-6pm
You will find: a large collection of estate and costume jewelry.

Walter's Flea Market
252 Bleeker St.   ☎ 255-0175
Hours: 10am-6pm daily.
You will find: primarily discounted new merchandise

Yorkville Flea Market
351 East 74th St.   ☎ 535-5235
Hours: Sat 9am-4pm (except June through August)
You will find: old china, jewelry, and coins.

THRIFT SHOPS

Big Apple Street Smarts: Most of the thrift shops sponsored by not-for-profit organizations are staffed by volunteers. They don't lose their jobs if they decide to close on Tuesday. Call to verify days, hours, and payment options (cash, check, credit cards). Depending on what arrived during the past few days, you may find either exactly what you want or nothing.

Cancer Care Thrift Shop
1480 Third Ave.   ☎ 879-9868
Clothing and furniture.

Dalton Vintage Emporium
156 East 86th St.   ☎ 831-4908
Books (some first editions), clothes, appliances, cameras and furniture.

Encore
1132 Madison Ave.   ☎ 879-2850
Clothes and jewelry.

Everybody's Thrift Shop
261 Park Ave. S.   ☎ 355-9263
Knickknacks, household goods, and appliances.

Exchange Unlimited
563 Second Ave.   ☎ 889-3229
Designer men's clothing and costume jewelry.

Girls Club of New York Thrift Shop
202 East 77th St.   ☎ 535-8570
Linen, napkins, and tablecloths, clothing.

Godmothers' League Thrift Shop
1457 Third Ave.   ☎ 988-2858
Clothes and furniture.

Irvington Institute for Medical Research Thrift Shop
1534 Second Ave.   ☎ 879-4555
Men's and women's clothes (vintage and contemporary), costume jewelry, china, silverware, and furniture.

Memorial Sloan Kettering Cancer Center Thrift Shop
1440 Third Ave.   ☎ 535-1250
Furniture selection includes pieces from the William Doyle Galleries. Many designer labels.

Michael's Resale Shop
1041 Madison Ave.   ☎ 737-7273
Major designer clothes.

New York Hospital Auxiliary Thrift Shop
439 East 71st St. ☎ 535-0965
Clothing, many brand names.

Renate's
217 East 83rd St. ☎ 472-1698
Designer clothes.

Second Act Children' Wear
1046 Madison Ave. ☎ 988-2440
Clothing, and baseball mitts to boots and belts.

Spence Chapin Corner Shop
1424 Third Ave. ☎ 737-8448
Clothing.

Thrift Shop East
336 East 86th St. ☎ 772-6868
Furniture and clothing.

Trishop
1689 First Ave. ☎ 369-2410
Most of the clothing is new, many designer labels.

GETTING IT THERE

Big Apple Street Smarts: At times neither the ☎ nor fax will suffice. Messenger services abound in the Big Apple. Federal Express, the United States Postal Service and others offer overnight services. You do not have to go to the post office to obtain information. 7 days a week an automated tele☎ information service is a ☎ call away.

HOW TO USE THE POSTAL SERVICE AUTOMATED INFORMATION SYSTEM

1. Look below for the message number for the information you want.

2. In the Big Apple, call 330-4000 on a touch-tone tele☎.

3. The recorded instructions will tell you when to push the buttons that correspond with your desired message number.

4. Wait a few moments for your message to begin.

5. For information on another service or to have the message repeated, wait for the tone, then press the appropriate message number.

Services that offer fast delivery.	Message No.
Express Mail®	132
Express Mail Next Day Service®	332
Express Mail Same Day Airport Service®	110
Express Mail Custom-Designed Service®	115
Express Mail International Service®	318
Where to deposit Express Mail® items	138
Special delivery	320
Special Handling	141

You need the location of a post office.	
Post office hours and locations	133
Self-service Postal centers	321

Information on other types of services.	
Which class of mail should I use?	333
First-Class Mail and Priority Mail rates	323
Second-Class Mail rates (newspapers and magazines)	336
Third-Class Mail and Bulk Business Mail rates (advertising and circulars)	322
Fourth-Class Parcel Post rates (packages)	122
Library rate	120
Special Fourth-Class Mail rate (books)	119

Rate calculations for mail services.

Express Mail - Post Office to Addressee
Up to 5 pounds 154
Express Mail - Post Office to Post Office
Up to 5 pounds 354
Express Mail Same Day Airport Service
Up to 5 pounds 302
Express Mail - Over 5 pounds - Call your
local post office for cost.

First Class Mail - Up to but not over
eleven (11) ounces 101
First Class Mail - Over 11 ounces, up to but
not over 32 ounces (2 pounds) 155
First Class Mail - Over 32 ounces, up to
80 ounces (5 pounds) 355
First-Class Mail - Over 80 ounces (5 pounds)
call your local post office for cost.

Parcel Post - Packages weighing up to but
not over fifteen pounds 301
Parcel Post--Packages weighing over fifteen
pounds - call your local post office.

When you send valuables or need proof of mailing or delivery.

How to send valuables through the mail Message No.

Registered mail 135
Insurance 337
How to file a claim for items lost or damaged
in the mail. 113

How to obtain proof of mailing or delivery
Certificate of mailing 111
Certified mail 121
Return receipt service (proof of delivery) 334

International mail.

Rates for First-Class surface mail 319
Airmail rates and information 134
Express Mail International Service 318
Parcel Post rates and information 317
Customs 308
Special services available 142
International Reply Coupons 307

How to send packages.

Which mailing option should I select? 310
Special services available for packages 143
How to prepare packages for mailing 139
Sending packages to the military 109

Resolving mail problems. Message No.

Mail Order.

73

Moving or Going On Vacation.

Fraud.

Security.

Miscellaneous

C.O.D.	112
Money orders	108
Passport applications	313
Post office boxes	316
	Message No.
Postage refunds and exchanges	341
Retention of undeliverable mail	342
Size standards for mail	118
Stamps by mail	107
ZIP + 4° coding: What is it?	389
Postal Service Reward Program	102
Local announcements	800
New messages since printing of this book	900

For Zip Code of an address call 967-8585.

Big Apple Street Smarts: If mailing on a Friday, and the letter or package doesn't have to arrive before Monday, Priority Mail is the cheapest of the "express services". It costs $2.90 for up to 2lbs ...anywhere in the United States. Use post office packaging since it is distinctive! Envelopes, rigid cardboard mailers, and boxes are available free! While it is not a guaranteed delivery it works 99 times out of 100!

Other Express Services

Federal Express ☎ 777-6500 Call for nearest location or pickup (available until about 8pm). The location open the latest, for next day delivery, is at 537 W. 33rd St. - get there before 9:45pm. There may be a line and they really mean 9:45pm.

DHL Worldwide Express ☎ 800-345-2727 for information and pickup.

United Parcel Service ☎ 695-7500 for information and pickup on next day air and second day air. Drop off is also possible at *Mail Boxes Etc. USA* stores.

FREE PUBLIC RESTROOMS

Big Apple Street Smarts:Enjoying a day in the Big Apple often necessitates a comfort stop. The following are some of the more pleasant and accessible spots. You don't need this book to tell you that the railroad and bus stations have restrooms. All the museums have restrooms, but unless it is a "free day" there is usually an admission fee. If you have weak kidneys, you may desire a comprehensive listing. Get a copy of Vicki Rovere's 52 page, Where To Go: A Guide To Mahanttan's Toilets.

The large "convention hotels", as opposed to smaller hotels, always have public bathrooms. They are usually above the lobby level on a floor marked "Meeting Rooms" or "Ballrooms". They are usually open all of the time. Most major department store restrooms are available 7 days a week, but store hours vary with the season.

Midtown

Avery Fisher Hall at Lincoln Center
Columbus & 64th St.
Hours: Daily 10am-11:30pm

Bergdorf Goodman
57th & 5th
West Side of 5th - restooms on 7th floor.
East Side of 5th - Men's on 3rd and women's on 2nd floor.

Bloomingdale's
59th & Lexington
Men's on 5th floor.
Women's on 4th and 7th floors.

Citicorp Center
153 East 53rd St.
Lower-level restrooms close at 8:30pm.

City University Graduate Center
between 33 West 42nd St. & 34 West 43rd St.

Crystal Pavillion
805 Third Ave., at 50th St.

Grand Hyatt Hotel
East 42nd St. - Next to Grand Central Station
Take escalator to Lobby Level or Conference Level

Hunter College Student Center.
Lexington Ave. at 68th St.

IBM Garden Plaza
590 Madison Ave. at 55th St.

Restrooms are on the lower level.

Lord & Taylor
5th Avenue at 38th St.
Men's restroom on the tenth floor
Women's restroom on the fifth floor

Macy's
34th St. & 6th Ave.
Men's on the 4th and 7th floors & in the Cellar Grill.
Women's on the 2nd, 6th, and 8th flrs. & in the Cellar Grill.

Marriott Marquis Hotel
1535 Broadway
The hotel has eight levels and each has its own restrooms.

New York Hilton
1335 Ave. Of The Americas
Take Escalator to 2nd floor meeting rooms level.

Olympic Tower
East 51st & 5th Ave.
In the passageway between 51st & 52nd St.

Park Avenue Plaza
55 East 52nd St.
Restrooms are locked. Ask the guard to let you in.

Parker Meridien Hotel
118 West 57th St.
Down one flight of steps at the end of the lobby.

Pierre Hotel
Fifth Ave., at 61st St.
Restrooms are on the second floor and near rotunda area.

RCA Building
30 Rockefeller Plaza
Restrooms are downstairs.

Saks Fifth Ave.
Men's restroom on the sixth floor
Women's restroom on the fourth floor

The Library and Museum for the Performing Arts
111 Amsterdam Ave. at Lincoln Center

The New York Public Library's Central Research Library
On Fifth Ave. between 40th and 42nd
Restroooms are on the third floor.

Tiffany's
Fifth Ave., at 57th St.
Restrooms are on the mezzanine guest level

Trump Tower
725 Fifth Ave., near 57th St.
Restrooms are downstairs near the cafe.

Waldorf Astoria Hotel
Park Ave., at 50th St.
Restrooms are on lobby level.

Downtown

City Hall
Broadway at Chambers
Women's on 2nd floor.
Men's at Council Chamber on 2nd floor & in basement.

New York State Supreme Court House
Foley Square - 60 Centre St.
Restrooms on 2nd floor.

United States Court House
Foley Square - 40 Centre St.
Restrooms Downstairs.

U.S. Custom House (now the Bankruptcy Court)
Below Bowling Green

Vista International Hotel
3 World Trade Center
Up the circular staircase.

Winter Garden - In the World Financial Center
Near the West St. entrance and in the adjoining Courtyard.

SPECIALIZED LIBRARIES

When you require in depth information on a topic, a specialized library may speed your search. The librarians will be familiar with your topic and render greater assistance than is ordinarily available in a general library. Phone to confirm days and hours.

American Craft Council Library
72 Spring Street   ☎ 274-0630
Hours: Tues., Wed., Fri. 1pm-5pm
Non-members must pay $5 per visit.
It has exhibition catalogues, magazines, and more than 3,500 volumes on American and International crafts since World War II.

American Museum of Natural History
Central Park West at 70th St.   ☎ 769-5400
Hours: Mon.-Fri. 11am-4pm, Wed till 7:30pm some Saturdays during school year 10am-3pm.
It has the largest reference library on natural history in the Western Hemisphere.

Cooper Hewitt Museum Library
2 East 91st St.   ☎ 860-6883
Hours: By appointment only, Mon.-Fri. 10am-5:30pm
The library has 40,000 to 50,000 volumes on furniture, textiles, and the decorative arts, as well as drawings and prints. Admission is free.

Horticultural Society of New York
128 West 58th St.   ☎ 757-0915
Hours: M-F 10am-6pm
It has information on every plant that grows. The public can use its library for reference.

Information Exchange of the Municipal Art Society
457 Madison Ave., near 50th St.   ☎ 980-1297
Hours: M-F 10am-1pm
Maintains files on subjects such as: buildings, traffic, water, historic preservation, Battery Park City, and the Times Square redevelopment project.

International Center of Photography
1130 Fifth Ave., at 94th St.   ☎ 860-1787
Hours: M-F 10am-6pm, closed 1-2pm for lunch.
Has a free library on the third floor.

Library of the Museum of American Folk Art
61 West 62nd St. (2 Lincoln Sq.)   ☎ 977-7170
Hours: By appointment only.
Extensive collection of works on quilts, portraits, wood carvings, and other examples of native and native art.

Mechanics & Tradesmen Library
20 West 44th St. ☎ 921-1767
Hours: Mon. - Thurs. 9am-6pm, Fri. till 5pm from April through
August. Closed in July. From September through March, Mon. -
Thurs. 9am-7pm , Fri. till 5pm. Regular membership, $25;
senior citizens and students, $10.
It houses more than 140,000 volumes-especially classics,
mysteries, history, and current fiction and nonfiction.

Metropolitan Museum of Art
Fifth Ave. at 82nd St. ☎ 535-7710
Hours: Sun.-Thurs. 9:30am-5:15pm., Fri.-Sat. 9:30am-8:45pm

Municipal Reference and Research Center
31 Chambers St., Room 112; ☎ 566-4282 Hours:
M-F 9am-4:30pm Everything published by every New York City
government agency is in the collection.

New York Academy of Medicine
2 East 103rd St. ☎ 876-8200
Hours: M-F 9am-5pm.

New York Genealogical and Biographical Society
122 East 58th St. ☎ 755-8532
Hours: M-Sat 9:30am-5pm (October-May); closed Sat in June,
July, and September, closed in August. Minimum $3 donation
requested from nonmembers.

New York Historical Society Library
170 Central Park West, at 77th St. ☎ 873-3400
Hours: T,W,F noon-5pm, Thurs. noon-8pm.

**New York Public Library Early Childhood Resource and
Information Center, ERIC**
66 Leroy St. ☎ 929-0815
Hours: Tues.-Fri. 1pm-6pm, Thurs. 1pm-8pm, Sat. 12pm-5pm.

New York Society Library
53 East 79th St. ☎ 288-6900
Hours: M,W,F,Sat. 9am-5pm, Tues. & Thurs. 9am-7pm.
More than 225,000 volumes of history, art, travel, biography,
and fiction. Membership: One-year household membership,
$100; six months, $65. Individual student or teacher, $40 for
one year.

Small Press Center
20 West 44th St. ☎ 764-7021
Hours: Same as Mechanics & Tradesmen Library. Reference
works on publishing and the works of small presses.

EATING IN

Big Apple Street Smarts: You can shop for food in almost every neighborhood of Manhattan 24 hours a day, 7 days a week. Korean greengrocers toil round the clock and stock everything from fruit and vegetables to cake and beer. Many have salad bars and sandwich counters. Some of the larger supermarkets remain open until midnight and a few are open 24 hours. If you crave fast food, you will find the usual assortment of hamburger and chicken franchises. Some are open 24 hours. Whether you live in the Big Apple or are a visitor residing at a hotel, you will find it less expensive to eat in. Depending on where you shop, you may even get gourmet meals for less than mediocre restaurant fare.

Editor's Picks - A Short List- Gourmet Quality

Balducci's
424 Avenue Of The Americas ☎ 673-2600
Meats and other specialties.

Citrella Market
2135 Broadway ☎ 874-0383
Fish and an artful window display.

D'Aiuto's Pastry
405 8th Ave. & 873 8th Ave. ☎ 564-7136
New York cheesecake at its best.

Dean & Deluca
121 Prince & 560 Broadway ☎ 254-8776
An emphasis on Italian treats plus other goodies. Large variety at premium prices.

Jefferson Market Inc.
455 Avenue Of The Americas ☎ 675-2277
Meats, seafood.

Lobel Brothers Prime Meats
1096 Madison Ave. ☎ 737-1372

Nevada Meat Market
2012 Broadway ☎ 362-0443

Zabar's
2245 Broadway ☎ 787-2000
From smoked fish, caviar, cheese, fresh ground coffee, to prepared food this is our favorite. Large variety at fair prices.

DINING OUT

Big Apple Street Smarts: Over 6,000 restaurants are listed in Yellow Pages of the Manhattan phone book. If you ate out, two meals a day, it would take 8½ years to eat in each. By the time you finished, there would be a few thousand new restaurants and many of those you sampled would have closed their doors.

If you are on a tight budget Gray's, on the southeast corner of Broadway & 72nd St. will feed you two grilled all beef hotdogs and a fruit drink for $2. On the northwest corner of Third Ave. & 86th St., the Papaya King will serve you the same meal for $3.

Chef's change, menu's change, and one person's "fantastic" is often your "you call this food!". Try our list or listen to the last person you heard rave about a restaurant. If it's not what you had your heart set on, there are 6,000 more to try!

Restaurants open, close, and move. After you select, call to verify location, hours, dress code, reservation policy, and which, if any, credit cards are accepted.

Type Of Food Key:

AF = Afghan, AM = American, BR = Brazilian, CA = Caribbean, CH = Chinese, CU = Cuban, DE = NY Deli
FR = French,   GK = Greek,   GM = German,   HN = Hungarian, IN = Indian, IT = Italian, JP = Japanese
ME = Middle   Eastern,   MI = Milanese,   MX = Mexican, RM = Roumanian, RS = Russian, SP = Spanish
SW = Swiss, TH = Thai, VE = Venetian

Price Range Key - most expensive item on menu.

$ = under $20.
$$ = $20-$30.
$$$ = over $30.

Big Apple smarts: With beverage, desert, tax and tip you will pay a total of between 2 and 2½ times the cost of the main course for your meal. Budget accordingly!

AF-Afghanistan Kebab House
764 Ninth Ave.   ☎ 307-1612
$

AM-America
9 East 18th St.   ☎ 505-2110
$

AM-Gallagher's Steak House
228 West 52nd St.   ☎ 245-5336
$$

AM-P.J. Clarke's
915 Third Ave.   ☎ 759-1650
$

AM-Papa Bear
210 East 23rd St.   ☎ 685-0727
$

AM-Sylvia's
328 Lenox Ave.   ☎ 996-0660
$

AM-The Coach House
110 Waverly Place   ☎ 777-0303
$$

AM-The Conservatory
15 Central Park West   ☎ 581-1293
$$

CA-Caribe
117 Perry St.   ☎ 255-9191
$

CH-Au Mandarin
200-250 Vesey St.   ☎ 385-0310
$$

CH-Bo Ky
80 Bayard St.   ☎ 406-2292
$

CH-Fu's
1395 2nd Ave.   ☎ 517-9670
$

CH-Shun Lee West
43 West 65th St.   ☎ 595-8895
$

CH-Tse Yang
34 East 51st St.   ☎ 688-5447
$

CU-Victor's Cafe
240 Columbus Ave.   ☎ 595-8599
$

DE-Carnegie Delicatessen
854 7th Ave.   ☎ 757-2245
$

DE-Second Avenue Kosher Delicatessen
156 Second Ave.   ☎ 677-0606
$

DE-Stage Delicatessen
834 7th Ave.   ☎ 245-7850
$

FR-L'Omnibus de Maxim's
680 Madison Ave.   ☎ 980-6988
$$

FR-La Colombe D'or
134 East 26th St.   ☎ 689-0666
$

FR-Lutece
249 East 50th St.   ☎ 752-2225
$$$

FR-Poiret
474 Columbus Ave.   ☎ 724-6880
$

FR-The Terrace
400 West 119 St.   ☎ 666-9490
$$

GK-Periyali
35 West 20th St.   ☎ 463-7890
$

GM-Kleine Konditorei Restaurant
234 East 86th St.   ☎ 737-7130
$

HN-Mocca Hungarian Restaurant
1588 Second Ave.   ☎ 734-6470
$

IN-Akbar Restaurant
475 Park Ave.   ☎ 838-1717
$

IN-Darbar
44 West 56th St.   ☎ 432-7227
$

IT-Carmine's Westside
2450 Broadway   ☎ 362-2200
$

IT-Maruzzella
1479 First Ave.   ☎ 988-8877
$

IT-Sfuzzi
58 West 65th St.   ☎ 873-3700
$

IT-Trattoria Dell's Arte
900 Seventh Ave.   ☎ 245-9800
$$

IT-Villa Mosconi
69 MacDougal St.   ☎ 673-0390
$

JP-Benihana, The Japanese Steakhouse
120 East 56th St.   ☎ 593-1627
$$

JP-Hatsuhana
17 East 48th St.   ☎ 355-3345
237 Park Ave.   ☎ 661-3400
$$

JP-Nishi NoHo
380 Lafayatte St.   ☎ 677-8401
$$

ME-Sido Abu Salim
81 Lexington Ave.   ☎ 686-2031
$

MI-Biricchino
260 West 29th St.   ☎ 695-6690
$

MX-El Parador
325 East 34th St.   ☎ 679-6812
$

MX-Miracle Grill
112 First Ave.   ☎ 254-2353
$

MX-Tortilla Flats
767 Washington St.
$ ☎ 243-1658

MX-Zarela
953 Second Ave.   ☎ 644-6740
$

RM-Triplets Roumanian
Sixth Ave. bet. Canal & Grand   ☎ 925-9303
$

RS-The Russian Tea Room
150 West 57th St.   ☎ 265-0947
$$$

SP-Ballroom
253 West 28th St.   ☎ 244-3005
$

SP-Harlequin
569 Hudson St.   ☎ 255-4950
$

TH-Tommy Tang's
323 Greenwich St.   ☎ 334-9190
$

VE-Arqua
281 Church St.   ☎ 334-1888
$$

MEDICAL ADVICE & INFORMATION BY PHONE

Big Apple Street Smarts: While there is no substitute for talking to a doctor who has your medical record and the opportunity to examine you and/or administer tests, there are times when you may desire or need information that is available at little or no cost by phone. One of the key services are the not-for-profit medical referral lines run by hospitals and medical societies. If you don't have a doctor, desire a second opinion, or want to change doctors, the referral lines are an excellent start.

Tel Med Service

Tel-Med is a telephone library offering tapes on medical and health topics which have been approved by Lenox Hill Hospital physicians. Select any title in the following listing, then dial (212)-439-3200. You will be guided through the system. If you have a touch tone phone, you can access programs without talking to the operator. The pre-recorded program, which runs from five to nine minutes, will then be played for you over the telephone.

Lenox Hill Hospital Tel-Med is a 24 hr-7 days a week service. It is free except for the cost of the local call.

Alcoholism
Alcoholism: scope of the problem	442
So you love an Alcoholic	445

Cancer: Seven Paths to Cancer Prevention: Sponsored by the American Cancer Society, NYC Division.
Seven Paths to Cancer Prevention	388
Diet and Cancer	391
Smoking and Cancer	392
Alcohol and Cancer	393
Stress and Cancer	394
Occupational Hazards and Cancer	385
Environmental Hazards and Cancer	386
Self-Examination and Cancer	387

Cancer: Sponsored by the American Cancer Society, NYC.
Breast Cancer	706
Breast Self-Examination	864
Cancer in Black Americans	635
Cancer of the Bladder	521
Cancer of the Brain	522
Cancer of the Larynx	523
Cancer of the Prostate Gland	176
Cancer of the Skin	185
Cancer of the Stomach	525
Childhood Leukemia	359
Colorectal Cancer	379

Doctor Referral Services

By calling the following numbers, you will be offered the names and phone numbers of doctors considered specialists by their colleagues. They have been screened by the sponsoring institution. The following are referral services which can be reached without going through the hospital switchboard.

Beth Israel Medical Center	☎ 420-4000
Beth Israel Hospital North	☎ 870-9262
Cabrini Medical Center	☎ 533-9140
Columbia- Presbyt. Medical Center	☎ 305-5156
Hospital For Joint Diseases	☎ 598-6727
Hospital For Special Surgery	☎ 606-1555
Lenox Hill Referral Service	☎ 439-2046
Mem. Sloan-Kettering Cancer	☎ 800-525-2225
Mount Sinai Medical Ctr.	☎ 800-MD-SINAI
New York County Medical Society	☎ 399-9048
New York Hospital	☎ 800-222-2NYH
St. Luke's-Roosevelt Hospital Center	☎ 876-5432
St. Vincent's Hospital & Med. Center	☎ 790-1111

Doctors By Phone

To talk to a doctor, 24 hours a day, dial 1-900-77Doctor". Calls are $3 per minute. You get to speak to a doctor who will answer your questions.

PDR® Prescription InfoLine™

To obtain facts about your prescription, 24 hours a day, ☎ 900-976-7771. Calls are $1.50 per minute. 2-to-5 minute recorded messages are provided on hundreds the most prescribed medicine. You learn acceptable dosage levels, warnings, side effects, conflicting drugs, and more.

ALL I WANT IS A ROOM SOMEWHERE

Big Apple Street Smarts: The majority of Manhattan hotel rates are geared to the business week. Prices are higher from Sunday night to Thursday night than on the weekend. The pricing is the opposite of resort area prices. You can often obtain a weekend rate which is a fraction of the business week rate. The rates at the following hotels are below those of the luxury hotels and the large convention hotels, but it can't hurt to inquire at the luxury hotels about the availability of weekend rates. Verify current rates when you call for reservations. A recent renovation or change in ownership may have resulted in an escalation of rates!

Hotels Under $100 per night.

Beekman Tower
First Ave. at 49th St.   ☎ 355-7300

Dumont Plaza
150 East 34th St.   ☎ 481-7600

Eastgate Tower
222 East 39th St.   ☎ 687-8000

Lyden Gardens
215 East 64th St.   ☎ 355-1230

Hotel Beverly
125 East 50th St.   ☎ 800-223-0945

Lyden House
320 East 53rd St.   ☎ 888-6070

Paramount
235 West 46th St.   ☎ 764-5500

Plaza Fifty
155 East 50th St.   ☎ 751-5710

Shelburne Murray Hill
303 Lexington Ave.   ☎ 689-5200

Southgate Tower
371 Seventh Ave.   ☎ 563-1800

Surrey Hotel
20 East 76th St.   ☎ 288-3700

The Milford Plaza Hotel
270 West 45th St.   ☎1-800-522-6449

You're not on a budget!

Grand Hyatt
42nd St. at Grand Central Station ☎ 883-1234

Inter-Continental New York
111 East-48th-St. ☎ 755-5900

Marriot Marquis
1535 Broadway ☎ 398 1900

Mayfair Regent
610 Park Ave. ☎ 288-0800

New York Hilton
1355 Avenue of the Americas ☎ 586-7000

New York Marriot Marquis
1335 Broadway ☎ 800-228-9290

Omni Bershire Place
21 East 52nd St. ☎ 753-5800

Parker Meridien
118 West 57th St. ☎ 245-5000

Peninsula New York
700 Fifth-Ave. ☎ 247-2200

Pierre
Fifth Ave. at 61st St. ☎ 838-8000

Plaza
Fifth Ave. at 59th St. ☎ 759-3000

Rihga Royal Hotel
151 West 54th St. ☎ 800-937-5454

The Carlyle
Madison Ave. at 76th St. ☎ 744-1600

The New York Vista Hotel
3 World-Trade-Center ☎ 800-258-2505

The Lowell
28 East 63rd St. ☎ 838-1400

The Mayfair Regent
610 Park Ave. ☎ 288-0800

YOUR HOMETOWN NEWSPAPER - MAGAZINES

Eastern Lobby Shop at the Pan Am Building
200 Park Ave. ☎ 687-1198
Hours: Mon.-Sat. 6am-10pm
Large selection of domestic magazines.

Hotaling's News Agency
142 West 42nd St. ☎ 840-1868,9
Hours: Mon.-Fri. 7:30am-9:00pm, Sat.-Sun. 10am-11:30pm.
Stocks 300+ out-of-town papers and 175 foreign papers.

Hudson News
265 East 66th St. ☎ 988-2683
Hours: Sun.-Thur. 10am-9pm, Fri.-Sat. 10am-11:30pm.
Political and literary journals along with many domestic and
foreign magazines with interest ranging from cars to
computers.

Librairie Lipton
850 Lexington Ave. ☎ 628-7600
Hours: Mon.-Sat. 9:30am-6pm
Large selection of domestic and foreign magazines, with an
emphasis on fashion.

Dina Magazines
270 Park Ave. South ☎ 674-6595
Hours: Mon.-Fri. 6am-10:30pm, Sat. 6am-12am, Sun. 7am-
7pm
Good selection of magazines and newspapers. Foreign
magazines are mainly Italian and French, and foreign
newspapers only European.

Nikos Smoke & Magazine Shop
462 Sixth Ave. ☎ 255-9175
Hours: Mon.-Fri. 7am-11pm, Sat. 7am-1pm, Sun. 7am-10pm
Many magazines and journals, some of which focus on the
arts, progressive groups, and controversial issues.

Rizzoli International Bookstore
31 West 57th St. ☎ 759-2424
Hours: Mon.-Sat. 9am-8pm, Sun. 12pm-8pm
Broad selection of foreign periodicals and European
newspapers.

SPECIALIZED BOOKSTORES

Big Apple Street Smarts: If you are looking for a best seller, your best bet is Barnes & Nobles. They discount every book and offer an extra large discount on the New York Times Bestseller List. Their stores are scattered around Manhattan with the two largest being at 600 Fifth and 105 Fifth Avenue. For out-of-print books and reviewer's copies of recent books, try the Strand Book Store, 828 Broadway.

Architecture & Design

Urban Center Books
457 Madison Ave. ☎ 935-3592

Art

Rizzoli Book Store
31 West 57th St. ☎ 759-2424

Rietman Jaap Inc.
134 Spring St. ☎ 966-7044

Business & Management

McGraw-Hill Bookstore
1221 Avenue Of The Americas ☎ 512-4100

Cooking & Gourmet Eating

Kitchen Arts & Letters Inc.
1435 Lexington Ave. ☎ 876-5550

Maps & Travel Guides

Hagstrom Map & Travel Center
57 West 43rd St. ☎ 398-1212

Rand McNally Map & Travel Store
150 East 52nd St. ☎ 758-7488

New York

New York Bound Bookshop
50 Rockefeller Plaza ☎ 245-8503

Photography

A Photographers Place
133 Mercer St. ☎ 431-9358

Theater

Applause Theater Books
211 West 71st St. ☎ 496-7511

Drama Book Shop, Inc.
723 7th Ave. ☎ 944-0595

If you don't see your specialty listed, try the *Manhattan Yellow Pages - Book Dealers: Guide of Book Dealers Arranged By Specialty*

● ● ●

BORROWING/RENTING BOOKS ON TAPE

Big Apple Street Smarts: If you are taking a long car trip, you may be bored by the local radio stations. Try borrowing or renting tapes to entertain yourself. Tapes are a thoughtful idea for those convalescing in a hospital or recuperating at home. Reading is often too much of an effort. To borrow from a library, you will need a library card. Call to ascertain hours. Budget cuts have caused many libraries to reduce the number of days and/or hours that they are open. Your neighborhood library may now have a collection. If you want to buy recorded tapes, you will find them at most bookstores and at some of the larger record stores.

Mid-Manhattan Library
Fifth Ave. at 40th St. ☎ 340-0837

Recorded Books
140 West 22nd St. ☎ 243-8070

Recorded Books
Clinton, M.D. ☎ 800-638-1304

The Donnell Library
20 West 53rd St. ☎ 621-0609

The Lincoln Center Library
65th St. and Amsterdam Ave. ☎ 870-1629

INSTANT OFFICES

Big Apple Street Smarts: If you are looking to establish your business in Manhattan without the hassle of leasing space, buying office furniture, and hiring a secretary, try one of the available packages. Packaged deals may even be less expensive than having your own office since you will be sharing a receptionist and switchboard. As you grow, the packaged deals become less cost efficient.

When looking for space, you will find that the cost of the same size office will vary from building to building and from one area of Manhattan to another. If your customers or clients don't visit your office, you should go for the best deal rather than the best address!

Corporate Executive Offices
599 Lexington Ave.   ☎ 836-4800

Empire State Communications
350 Fifth Ave.   ☎ 736-8072

Executive Systems International, Ltd.
One Dag Hammarskjold Plaza   ☎ 758-6400

521 Fifth Ave. Service Co.
521 Fifth Ave.   ☎ 682-5844

HQ-Headquarters Companies
237 Park Ave.   ☎ 949-0722
53 Wall St.   ☎ 558-6400
237 Park Ave.   ☎ 949-0722
666 Fifth Ave.   ☎ 541-3800
1120 Avenue Of The Americas   ☎ 840-1199

Maruko New York, Inc.
9 East 45th St.   ☎ 972-0505

Pedus Office
885 Third Ave.   ☎ 230-2323

Penn Plaza Service Associates
2 Penn Plaza   ☎ 244-3247

World Trade Center Executive Offices
One World Trade Center   ☎ 524-0400

World-Wide Business Centers
575 Madison Ave.   ☎ 977-3152

PROFESSIONAL HELP

Big Apple Street Smarts: Picking a doctor or a lawyer from the phone book is a form of Russian Roulette. Use one of the referral services provided by professional associations. If you have a deep pocket, you can contact one of the major players. The Legal Aid Society has income ceilings for persons they assist.

Until the 1980's, there were legal specialties that were deemed unsuitable for the large "white shoe" firms. They included criminal law and bankruptcy. Now almost all large firms do white collar crime and have bankruptcy departments. Divorce, street crime, patent, copyright, trademark, and plaintiff negligence law remain primarily in the domain of smaller "boutique" firms.

Accountants - no association sponsored referral service.

Attorneys: Association of the Bar   ☎ 382-6625
           Legal Aid Society - Civil   ☎ 227-2755
           Legal Aid Society - Criminal   ☎ 577-3355

Dentists: Dental Society   ☎ 889-8940

Doctors: N.Y. County Medical Society Panel   ☎ 399-9048

Law Firms For Those With Deep Pockets

Ask for the Managing Partner if you don't know the name of the attorney you want to speak to.

Skadden, Arps, Slate, Meagher & Flom
919 Third Ave.   ☎735-3000

Shearman & Sterling
153 E. 53rd   ☎ 848-4000

Accounting Firms For Those With Deep Pockets

KPMG Peat Marwick
345 Park Ave.   ☎ 758-9700

Delotte & Touche
1 World Trade Center   ☎ 669-5000

FOREIGN BANK BRANCHES IN MANHATTAN

*Big Apple Street Smarts: When doing business overseas,
transferring money, or traveling, it may be convenient to use
the services of a Big Apple branch of a foreign bank. Your own
bank will probably have a branch in a major capital, but what
about the small town where your family comes from?*

Algemene Bank Nederland N.V. - Netherlands
335 Madison Ave.   ☎ 503-2400

Banca Nazionale del Lavoro - Italy
25 West 51st St.   ☎ 581-0710

Banca Commerciale Italiana - Italy
1 William St.   ☎ 607-3500

Banco di Roma-Italy
100 Wall St.   ☎ 952-9300

Banco de Santander S.A. - Spain
375 Park Ave.   ☎ 826-4350

Banco di Napoli - Italy
277 Park Ave.   ☎ 644-8400

Bank Leumi - Israel
120 Broadway   ☎ 912-6262

Bank of Montreal - Canada
430 Park Ave.   ☎ 758-6300

Banque Nationale de Paris - France
499 Park Ave.   ☎ 750-1400

Banque Indosuez - France
1230 Sixth Ave.   ☎ 408-5600

Barclays Bank PLC - England
75 Wall St.   ☎ 412-4000

Commerzbank Aktiengesellschaft - Germany
55 Broad St.   ☎ 208-6200

Credit Suisse - Switzerland
100 Wall St.   ☎ 612-8000

Credit Lyonnais - France
95 Wall St.   ☎ 344-0500

Dai-ichi Kangyo Bank Ltd. - Japan
One World Trade Center #4911   ☎ 466-5260

Daiwa Bank Ltd. - Japan
75 Rockefeller Plaza ☎ 480-0300

Deutsche Bank - Germany
31 West 52nd St. ☎ 474-8000

Fuji Bank Ltd. - Japan
Two World Trade Center ☎ 898-2400

Generale Bank - Belgium
520 Madison Ave. ☎ 418-8700

Industrial Bank of Japan Ltd. - Japan
245 Park Ave. ☎ 557-3535

Korea First Bank - Korea
410 Park Ave. ☎ 593-2525

Lloyds Bank PLC - England
199 Water St. ☎ 607-4300

Mitsui Trust & Bank Co. - Japan
200 Liberty St. ☎ 341-0200

Monte dei Paschi di Siena - Italy
245 Park Ave. ☎ 557-8111

National Bank of Canada - Canada
125 West 55th St. ☎ 632-8500

National Westiminster Bank PLC - England
175 Water St. ☎ 602-1000

Societe Generale - France
50 Rockefeller Plaza ☎ 830-6600

Standard Chartered Bank PLC - England
160 Water St. ☎ 269-3100

Sumitomo Bank Ltd. - Japan
One World Trade Center #9651 ☎ 553-0100

Svenska Handelsbanken PLC - Sweden
599 Lexington Ave. ☎ 326-5100

Swiss Bank Corp. - Switzerland
Four World Trade Center ☎ 574-3000

Toronto-Dominion Bank - Canada
31 West 52nd St. ☎ 468-0300

Union Bank of Switzerland - Switzerland
299 Park Ave. ☎ 715-3000

EXERCISE, HEALTH & FITNESS CLUBS

Big Apple Street Smarts: Exercise and fitness comes at a price. It may vary from the nominal cost of running shoes for joggers to several thousand dollars in membership dues and fees at a commercial, private, or not-for-profit club. The factors to be considered include location (near your residence or work), hours, whether a pool is important to you, whether it has an indoor track, equipment, personnel, and the social milieu. Many facilities offer trial or introductory memberships. Discounts offered for prepayment of multiyear memberships may not be a bargain, if the club closes within the time frame of your membership.

92nd St. Y
1395 Lexington Ave.   ☎ 415-5700
Equipment: Nautilus circuit, Universal, free weights, Biocycles, cross-country machines, treadmills, Liferowers, Monarch ergometers, Stairmasters, Gravitron.
Facilities, Programs, & Classes: pool, running track, eight racquetball courts, basketball, saunas, steam, massage, one-on-one training, in-house exercise physiologist, stress testing, nutritional counseling, coronary program, classes include: aerobics, low-impact aerobics, stretch and firm slimnastics, yoga, martial arts, self-defense, boxing, weight training, infant gym and swimming programs, prenatal and postpartum exercise programs, exercise for mothers, with babysitting.

Alex and Walter
30 West 56th St.   ☎ 265-7270
Facilities, Programs, & Classes: Four studios, free weights, parallel bars, rings trapeze, tumbling mats, dressing rooms, showers, classes include: gymnastics and low-impact aerobics.

Apple Health & Sports Club
321 East 22nd St.   ☎ 673-3730
Reciprocal membership with other Apple clubs.
Equipment: Nautilus machines, Stairmasters, Lifecycles, treadmills, Versa Climber, Concept II ergometers.
Facilities, Programs, & Classes: pool, sauna, steam, whirlpool, sun deck, tanning, massage, on-on-one training.

Apple Health & Sports Club
1438 Third Ave.   ☎ 879-5400
Reciprocal membership with other Apple clubs.
Equipment: Nautilus, Universal, and Olympic circuits, Olympic and regular free weights, Lifecycles, Concept II rowing machines, Versa Climbers, Quiton treadmills, Stairmaster 4000.
Facilities, Programs, & Classes: pool, sauna, steam, whirlpool, tanning, massage, aerobics classrooms, one-on-one training, sports-injury-rehabilitation clinic.

Apple Health & Sports Club
211 Thompson St. ☎ 777-4890
Equipment: Nautilus circuit, Olympic free weights:
Stairmasters, Lifecycles, Concept II rowing machines, Quinton
treadmills.
Facilities, Programs, & Classes: pool, sauna, steam, whirlpool,
massage, tanning, sun deck, exercise classrooms, one-on-one
training.

Apple Health & Sports Club
88 Fulton St. ☎ 227-7450
Reciprocal membership with other Apple clubs.
Equipment: Nautilus circuit, Olympic free weights, Versa
Climbers, Lifecycles, Stairmasters, Quinton treadmills, rowing
machines.
Facilities, Programs, & Classes: pool, racquetball court, sauna,
steam, whirlpool, tanning, sun deck, massage, exercise
classrooms, cardiovascular room, one-on-one training.

Athletic Complex
3 Park Ave. ☎ 686-1085
Equipment: Eagle Cybex circuit, free weights, upper-body
ergometer, Lifecycles, computerized treadmills, rowing
machine, Stairmasters.
Facilities, Programs, & Classes: squash court, sauna, massage,
juice bar, lounge, aerobics classes, self-defense classes, one-
on-one fitness training, physical therapist on premises.

Back in shape with Marjorie Jaffe
37 West 54th St. ☎ 245-9131
Facilities: studio, changing room, showers, classes include:
gymnastics and low-impact aerobics.

Battery Park Swim & Fitness Center at Gateway Plaza
375 South End Ave. ☎ 321-1117
Equipment: Combined Nautilus and Eagle circuit, free weights,
treadmills, Lifecycles, Stairmaster, rowing ergometers, cross-
country machines.
Facilities, Programs, & Classes: pool, sauna, steam, whirlpool,
tanning(solaria and sun deck), massage, Aquasize programs,
scuba diving, aerobics, and yoga, one-on-one exercise
instruction, medical testing.

Body Formula Inc.
305 East 92nd St. ☎ 860-7321
Facilities, Programs, & Classes: Mirrored studio, Dressing room,
shower.
Classes: Low-and high-impact aerobics, pain-free back and
neck exercises, dyna-band workouts, prenatal and post-partum
exercises, fitness for kids.

Bodyworks Fitness Center
626 Broadway ☎ 475-5030
Equipment: Nautilus circuit, free weights, bicycles, rowing
ergometers, cross-country machine, treadmill, Lifecycles, Versa
Climber, Stairmaster.

Facilities, Programs, & Classes: massage and bodywork, classes include low-impact aerobics, abdominal workshop, t'ai chi, yoga, kung fu, self-defense, stretch.

Cardio-Fitness Center
79 Maiden Lane   ☎ 943-1510
Reciprocal membership with Cardio-Fitness Centers in Pan Am Building, 345 Park Ave., 9 West 57th St., and 1221 Ave. of the Americas.
Equipment: Universal machines, Stairmasters, free weights, bicycles, Concept II rowing machines, treadmills, aerobics-exercise equipment.
Facilities, Programs, & Classes: sauna, individualized programs, cardiovascular evaluation.

Chelsea Gym (Men)
267 West 17th St.   ☎ 255-1150
Equipment: Nautilus machines, Icarian free weights and other equipment, stationary bicycles.
Facilities, Programs, & Classes: sauna, steam room, massage, tanning, sun deck, health bar, pro shop, fitness evaluation, nutritional and exercise counseling, one-on-one training, endurance, abdominal, and aerobics classes.

Club La Raquette (in Le Parker Meridien Hotel)
119 West 56th St.   ☎ 245-1144
Equipment: Nautilus circuit, dumbbells, Stairmasters, Liferowers, Lifecycles, treadmills, bicycles, rowing machines.
Facilities, Programs, & Classes: pool, four racquetball courts, two squash courts, racquetball and squash pros, basketball court, volleyball court, sauna, whirlpool, sun deck, massage, one-on-one training.

Doral Saturnia Fitness Center
90 Park Ave.   ☎ 370-9692
Equipment: Nautilus and Eagle machines, free weights, computerized treadmills, Fitron bicycles, upper-body ergometers, Nordic Track, Versa Climbers, Stairmasters, rowing ergometers, Liferowers.
Facilities, Programs, & Classes: cardiovascular evaluation, personalized programs, one-on-one training.

Doral Inn Racquet and Fitness Training Center (a TSI Club)
541 Lexington Ave.   ☎ 838-2102
Reciprocal use of TSI clubs.
Equipment: Nautilus and Eagle fitness center, treadmills, Stairmasters, Lifecycles, Versa climbers, cross-country machines, rowing machines, aerobic equipment.
Facilities, Programs, & Classes: three squash courts, sauna, one-on-one training.

Eastside Sportsmedicine Center
244 East 84th St.   ☎ 570-0209
Equipment: Nautilus and Eagle circuits, free weights, Concept II rowing machines, upper body ergometers, downhill and cross-country machines, bicycles, treadmills.
Facilities, Programs, & Classes: personalized, monitored programs, cardiovascular evaluation, one-on-one training.

Equinox Fitness Club
344 Amsterdam Ave.   ☎721-4200
Equipment: Everything - the Westside's newest.
Facilities, Programs, & Classes: personalized, monitored programs

Executive Fitness Center (Vista International Hotel)
3 World Trade Center   ☎ 466-9266
Equipment: Nautilus and Keiser circuits, Universal machines, free weights, bicycles, cross-country machines, rowing machines, treadmill, Stairmaster.
Facilities, Programs, & Classes: pool, track, two racquetball courts, sauna, steam, massage, personalized programs, progress reviewed daily, on-on-one training, cardiovascular evaluation.

Fifth Ave. Racquet & Fitness Club
404 Fifth Ave.   ☎ 594-3120.
Reciprocal use of TSI clubs.
Equipment: Nautilus and Eagle circuits, free weights, treadmills, Stairmasters, Lifecycles, Gravitron, cross-country machines, rowing machines.
Facilities, Programs, & Classes: four squash courts, pro shop, sauna, massage, aerobic studio, juice bar, lounge, one-on-one training, daily aerobics classes.

Health Club at United Nations Plaza Hotel
First Ave. and East 44th St.   ☎ 702-5016
Equipment: training room with Universal gym, free weights, treadmills, bicycles, Concept II rowing machine, Stairmaster.
Facilities, Programs, & Classes: pool, tennis court, sauna.

Joy of Movement Dance and Fitness Center
400 Lafayette St.   ☎ 260-0453
Equipment: Nautilus circuit, free weights, Lifecycles, rowing machines.
Facilities, Programs, & Classes: three studios, sauna, classes include: high-and low-impact aerobics, stretch and tone, abdominal and thighs, ballet, ballroom modern, jazz, African-Haitian, t'ai chi, bodyworks, yoga

Lincoln Racquet & Fitness Club
61 West 62nd St.   ☎ 265-0995
Reciprocal use of other TSI clubs.
Equipment: Nautilus circuit, free weights, treadmills, Stairmasters, Lifecycles, Versa Climbers, cross-country machines, rowing machines.

Facilities, Programs, & Classes: five squash courts, sauna, juice bar, one-on-one training.

Manhattan Sports Club
335 Madison Ave. ☎ 983-5320
Equipment: Nautilus, Universal, Eagle, and Paramount circuits, Keiser, Icarian, Polaris, Body Masters, Olympic free weights, Lifecycles, Liferowers, Life Circuit, Versa Climbers, Stairmasters, UBE ergometers, Gravitron
Facilities, Programs, & Classes: pool, track, steam, sauna, whirlpool, health bar, daily aerobics classes.

McBurney YMCA
215 West 23rd St. ☎ 741-9210
Equipment: Nautilus and Universal circuits, free weights, bicycles, rowing machines, boxing equipment.
Facilities, Programs, & Classes: pool, track, three handball courts, basketball, volleyball, saunas, steam, sun deck, massage, fitness assessment, classes include: low-impact aerobics, calisthenics, stretch, water exercise, lower-back exercise, judo, karate, self-defense, weight training, prenatal exercise.

New York Body Designers
158 West 23rd St. ☎ 645-3687
Facilities, Programs, & Classes: Nautilus circuits, Lifecycles, Cybex Fitrons, Versa Climber, Concept II rower, fitness evaluation, classes include: all one-on-one, strength training based on Nautilus principles.

New York Health & Racquet Club
1433 York Ave. ☎ 737-6666
Reciprocal use of other HRC clubs and Village Tennis Courts.
Equipment: Nautilus and Eagle circuits, free weights, Stairmasters, Lifecycles, Liferowers, treadmills.
Facilities, Programs, & Classes: pool, sauna, steam, whirlpool, tanning, massage, two exercise classrooms, individualized programs, one-on-one training, nutritional counseling.

New York Health & Racquet Club
110 West 56th St. ☎ 541-7200
Reciprocal use of other HRC clubs and Village Tennis Courts.
Equipment: Nautilus equipment, Smith and Eagle machines, free weights, Stairmasters, Lifecycles, Lifecircuit, Liferowers, Gravitron, Versa Climber, treadmills.
Facilities, Programs, & Classes: pool, track, four racquetball courts, pro shop, three exercise classrooms, sauna, eucalyptus room, steam, whirlpool, tanning, massage, individualized programs, one-on-one training, nutritional counseling.

New York Health & Racquet Club
39 Whitehall St. ☎ 269-9800

Equipment: Eagle machines, Keiser k300 series, Nautilus circuit, free weights, Versa Climber, Lifecycles, Gravitron, Stairmaster, Liferowers, Treadmills.

Facilities, Programs, & Classes: pool, indoor track, racquetball and squash courts, steam, sauna, tanning, whirlpool, massage, two exercise studios, individualized programs, one-on-one training, nutritional counseling.

New York Health & Racquet Club
24 East 13th St.   ☎ 924-4600
Reciprocal use of other HRC clubs and Village Tennis Courts.
Equipment: Nautilus, Smith, and eagle machines, free weights, Lifecycles, treadmills.
Facilities, Programs, & Classes: pool, sauna, steam, whirlpool, tanning, massage, health-food bar, individualized programs, one-on-one training, nutritional counseling.

New York Health & Racquet Club
132 East 45th St.   ☎ 986-3100
Reciprocal use of other HRC clubs and Village Tennis Courts.
Equipment: Nautilus and Eagle circuits, Smith machines, free weights, Lifecycles, Stairmasters, Gravitron, Versa Climber, Liferowers.
Facilities, Programs, & Classes: pool, sauna, eucalyptus sauna, steam, whirlpool, tanning, massage, two exercise classrooms, one-on-one training; nutritional counseling.

New York Health & Racquet Club
20 East-50th St.   ☎ 593-1500
Reciprocal use of other HRC clubs and Village Tennis Courts.
Equipment: Smith and Eagle machines, Nautilus equipment, free weights, Lifecycles, Stairmasters, Gravitron, Versa Climber, upper-body ergometers, computerized treadmills, Liferowers.
Facilities, Programs, & Classes: pool, two squash courts, three exercise classrooms, sauna, eucalyptus sauna, steam, whirlpool, tanning, massage, individualized programs, one-on-one training, nutritional counseling.

Paris Health Club
752 West End Ave.   ☎ 749-3500
Equipment: Nautilus and Eagle machines, free weights; Stairmasters, Lifecycles, Windracer rowing machines.
Facilities, Programs, & Classes: pool, sauna, eucalyptus room, steam, two whirlpools, tanning, massage, three exercise studios, cafe, beauty and nutrition consultants.

Pollan-Austen Fitness Center
1487 First Ave.   ☎ 535-3300
Facilities, Programs, & Classes: studio with sprung-hardwood floor, dressing rooms, showers, classes include impact and low-impact aerobics, aerobic weight training combined with intensive sports drills, cardio rock.

Printing House Fitness & Racquet Club
421 Hudson St.   ☎ 243-7600
Equipment: Nautilus and Universal machines, free weights, treadmills, Liferowers, Concept II rowers, cross country machines, Lifecycles, upper-body ergometers.
Facilities, Programs, & Classes: outdoor pool with sun deck, five racquetball courts, four squash courts, pro shop, two racquet pros, sauna, steam, whirlpool, aerobic-dance studio, cafe and juice bar, personalized, supervised exercise programs; cardiovascular evaluation, weight-loss program, one-on-one training, sports-medicine department with physical therapy and sports-podiatry services.

Radu's
41 West 5th St.   ☎ 759-9617
Equipment: Universal machines, free weights, treadmills, pulleys, rings, tumbling floor, boxing equipment, rowers, bicycles, turbotrainers, Nordic Track ski machine, karate equipment.
Facilities, Programs, & Classes: One-on-one training; fitness evaluation, classes include: calisthenics, body toning, overall-fitness workout.

Sports Training Institute
239 East 49th St.   ☎ 752-7111
Equipment: Nautilus, Keiser, and Eagle machines, free weights, aerobic, cross-country, and rowing machines, Versa Climber, Stairmaster, treadmills, PTS Turbo bicycle, upper-body ergometers.
Facilities, Programs, & Classes: exercise area, cardiovascular training, personalized program, one-on-one training.

The Trainer's Edge
1568 Second Ave.   ☎ 517-4904
Equipment: Paramount weight-training equipment, free weights, Monarch bicycles, Concept II rowers, Nordic Track cross-country machine, treadmills, mini-trampolines.
Facilities, Programs, & Classes: massage, cardiovascular exercise, calisthenics, body toning, weight training, plyometrics, bodybuilding, fitness evaluation, nutrition counseling, pregnancy-fitness program.

The Vertical Club
330 East 61st St.   ☎ 355-5100
Equipment: Nautilus, Universal, and Keiser circuits; Olympic weights, Icarian, Versa Climber, Gravitron, Paramount, and Eagle equipment, Lifecycles, bicycles, cross-country machines. Liferowers, Stairmaster.
Facilities, Programs, & Classes: pool, track, five squash courts, three racquetball courts, steam, sauna, whirlpool, rooftop sun deck, exercise classroom, restaurant, tennis courts.

TSI Fitness Training Center/Arthro-Fitness Center
614 Second Ave.　☎ 213-5999
Reciprocal use of TSI clubs.
Equipment: Nautilus and Eagle circuits, free weights, treadmills,
Stairmasters, Lifecycles, Versa Climbers, cross-country
machines, rowing machines.
Facilities, Programs, & Classes: pool, whirlpool, sauna, sun
deck, aerobic studio, one-on-one training, physical therapy,
physical and hydrotherapy classes.

Uptown Racquet and Fitness Club
151 East 86th St.　☎ 860-8630
Reciprocal use of other TSI clubs.
Equipment: Nautilus circuits, free weights, treadmills,
Stairmasters, Lifecycles, Versa Climbers, cross-country
machines, Gravitron, rowing machines.
Facilities, Programs, & Classes: seven squash courts, pro shop,
sauna, sun dec, two aerobic studios, physical therapy, one-on-
one training.

West Side YMCA
5 West 63rd St.　☎ 787-4400
Equipment: Nautilus, Universal, Eagle circuits; free weights;
Heartmate bicycles, treadmills; boxing equipment.
Facilities, Programs, & Classes: two pools, track, two gyms,
two squash courts, four handball courts, strength training
center; saunas, steam, massage; one-on-one training, classes
include: aerobics, bodytone, weight training, calisthenics,
martial arts, yoga, boxing, wrestling.

Women's Mid-City Gym (women only)
224 West 4th St.　☎ 807-0025
Equipment: Weight-resistance machines redesigned for women,
cable equipment, free weights, bicycles, rowing machine,
Stairmaster, cross-country ski machines.
Facilities, Programs, & Classes: stretching area, steam, sauna,
massage, sun roof, health bar.　One-on-one training,
personalized instruction, nutritional counseling.

YWCA
610 Lexington Ave.　☎ 735-9755
Equipment: Universal circuit, free weights, treadmills, Nordic
Track, Stairmasters, rowing machines, upper-body ergometers,
bicycles.
Facilities, Programs, & Classes: pool, teaching pool, track (28
laps to the mile), Swedish massage, yoga, t'ai chi, judo, tennis,
one-on-one training, fitness testing, mammography testing.
Classes: aerobics, calisthenics, jazz exercise, back care,
exercise for pregnant women, swimming, first-aid, CPR.

BIBLIOGRAPHY

Periodicals

AT & T Toll-Free 800 Directory: annual issued in Consumer and Business editions - AT & T, Bridgewater, NJ - these directories should be definitive but unfortunately do not list all toll free numbers.

New York Magazine: a weekly - articles about New York City. It has complete theatre, movie, music, dance, nightlife, museum, and art gallery listing. Its *Activities For Children* section is a bonus for parents and grandparents.

The New York Times: The Sunday "Arts & Entertainment" contains theatre, museum, and art gallery listings. A complete movie guide is in the Friday Edition. The Sunday edition contains a separate "Television" section which lists both regular and cable programs.

Books

Knapp, Fred D., *The Complete Public Records Guide: Southern New York Region*, REyn, Inc., New Rochelle, NY, 1991. A detailed guide, complete with room diagrams, to all of the public records in New York City, Nassau, Suffolk, Westchester, Putnam, and Orange Counties. If you want to find the identity of building owners, the names of plaintiffs and defendants, you can hire a search firm, log onto some of the computerized systems, or do it yourself with this book, a pencil, change for copying machines, and a pad.

The Green Book, The Official Directory of The City of New York , Citybooks, 61 Chambers St. or by mail from Room 2223 Municipal Building, New York, NY 10007, published annually. A complete listing of city agencies, courts, independent agencies, state and federal agencies with phone numbers and addresses. It also tells you if you need a license for a particular business or activity.

Zagat New York City Restaurant Survey, New York, NY, published annually. Provides the results of a survey of regular restaurant goers of nearly 1,000 restuarants - indexed by type of cuisine, neighborhood location, special categories e.g. vegetarian, kosher, entertainment, with details on cusine, price range, and credit card policy. A favorite of Big Apple residents seeking eating adventures.

INDEX

117

Please help make *Big Apple Street Smarts* smarter.

● Send us the name and phone number of your favorite service, complaint, information or hot line so that we may include it in our next edition.

● If you have discovered that one of the phone numbers included in this edition has changed please tell us.

● If you have a topic that you would like to have included please let us know.

Mail your *smarts* to: The Consultant Press
163 Amsterdam Ave. #201
New York, NY 10023

Or fax it to: (212) 873-7065. Like the Big Apple, our fax never sleeps.